DEDICATED TO ALL MILITARY BRATS

ISBN: 9781657240148

TABLE OF CONTENTS

THE WALL

Mithras, God of the Morning, our trumpets waken the Wall!
"Rome is above the Nations, but Thou art over all!"
Now as the names are answered, and the guards are marched away,
Mithras, also a soldier, give us strength for the day!

Mithras, God of the Noontide, the heather swims in the heat,
Our helmets scorch our foreheads; our sandals burn our feet.
Now in the ungirt hour—now ere we blink and drowse,
Mithras, also a soldier, keep us true to our vows!

Mithras, God of the Sunset, low on the Western main—
Thou descending immortal, immortal to rise again!
Now when the watch is ended, now when the wine is drawn,
Mithras, also a soldier, keep us pure till the dawn!

Mithras, God of the Midnight, here where the great bull dies,
Look on Thy children in darkness. Oh take our sacrifice!
Many roads Thou hast fashioned all of them lead to the Light,
Mithras, also a soldier, teach us to die aright!

– Rudyard Kipling, A Song to Mithras
Hymn of the XXX Legion: circa AD 350

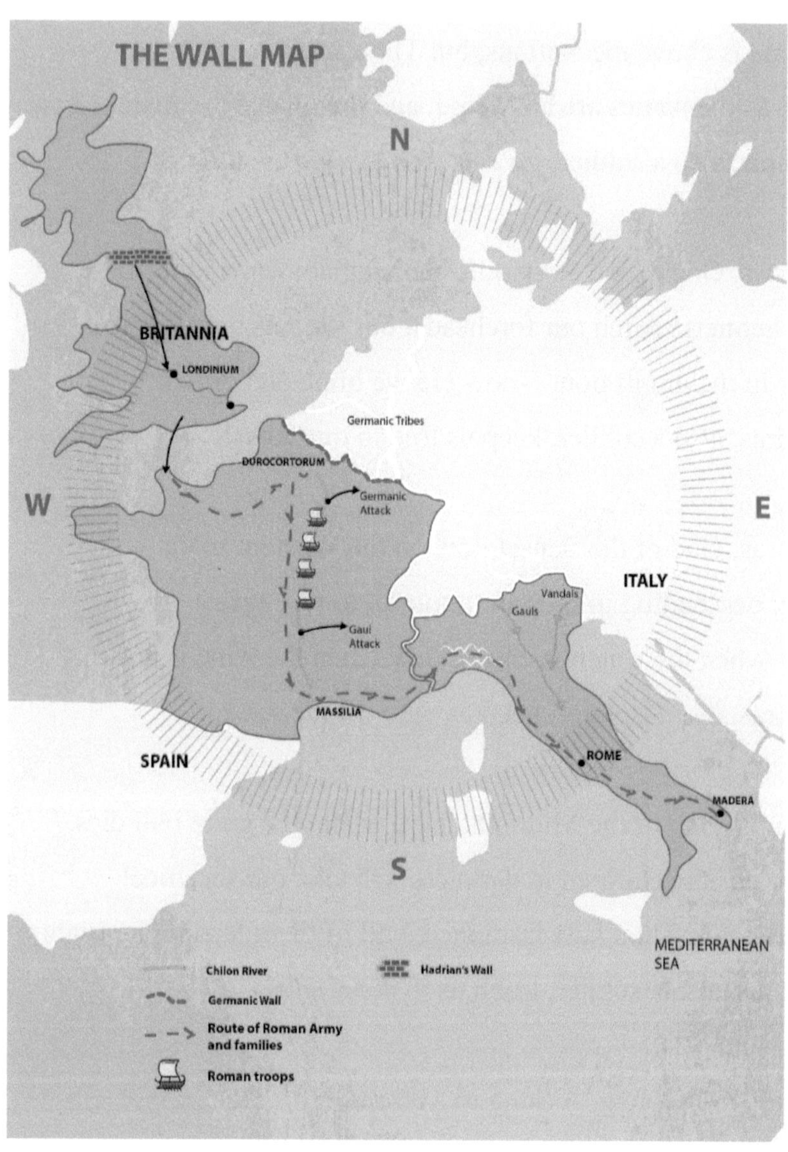
THE WALL MAP
N
W
E
S
BRITANNIA
LONDINIUM
Germanic Tribes
DUROCORTORUM
Germanic Attack
Gaul Attack
ITALY
Vandals
Gauls
MASSILIA
SPAIN
ROME
MADERA
MEDITERRANEAN SEA
Chilon River
Hadrian's Wall
Germanic Wall
Route of Roman Army and families
Roman troops

NORTH ENGLAND, HADRIAN'S WALL, JUNE AD 410

The border night was pitch black except for the stars above. A howl of wolves could be heard far away. A Roman soldier in a watchtower warmed his hands over the dying embers of a brazier, while nearby another guard finished pissing over the wall, adjusted his cloak, and walked back to the watch tower.

In the thick of trees, not so far away, another man sat hidden with his face painted blue and holding a javelin. He sat there, patiently watching the guards, counting who came and who went and at what phase of the moon. Two fresh guards approached the tired guards, exchanged grunts, salutes, and changed guard. Everyone was tired.

The clouds moved and exposed the moon as it moved over the sky and illuminated a rider on horseback coming from the south, who quickly approached the Wall's gates. He stopped his horse and called out to the guards his reason for coming, "Message from Rome, open the gates!"

The gates were opened by guards, and he rode into the center court of the fort and dismounted. A guard greeted him and took control of the horse as the rider dismounted. The rider walked over to the commander's quarters where a servant greeted him. As he entered the office, the old servant stopped him and bid him to wait. Quickly, the old servant knocked loudly on the door of the commander's private quarters. He then entered with a candle in one hand as he moved towards the sleeping figures of Commander Alban, and his wife, Julia.

The room contained a table, four chairs, and armor hanging nearby. A small wooden altar stood in one corner with offerings to Coventina, the Goddess thought to bring good fortune, along with incense and some food. Stacks of scrolls on racks lined one side of the wall.

The servant shook the sleeping man and whispered, "Commander Alban, sorry to awake you."

Waking up, the commander rubbed the sleep from his eyes. "What is it?" he demanded.

"A messenger rider has arrived with an important message from Rome, Sire," the servant replied, whispering. The Commander slowly got out of bed. The servant put the candle down on the table and moved to get the commander's tunic and helped him put it on.

"Alright, bring him in," the commander said as he adjusted his tunic and cloak. The servant soon came back with the messenger. The messenger saluted to the now sitting commander, who returned the salute. The servant busied himself with the lighting of more candles then stood behind the messenger.

The commander looked at the tired messenger and asked, "Where did you come from soldier and why at night?"

"I came from Aquae Arnemetiae, sir. I received the message from a rider from Londinium and was ordered to come right away, sir. The message comes directly from Rome and was sent in haste, sir."

The messenger passed the scroll to the commander. Commander Alban broke the seal, read the message, rubbed his face up and down, then put the scroll on the table. Looking past the messenger, he ordered, "Servant, take this man to get some food and get cleaned up. Bring him back here in one hour. Wake up Centurion Marcus and bring him here...and bring us something to eat and drink."

The servant bowed and taking the messenger by the arm, escorted him out of the room. A few minutes later, Centurion Marcus came into the room, wearing only his tunic and robe. He was an imposing man; tall, well-built, with a battle scar on his right cheek. He yawned "A bit early for breakfast, no?"

"Yes, it is Marcus. Have a seat," the commander replied. The centurion pulled up a chair and sat down. The servant came back in with a light breakfast of cheese and bread on plates, laid them on the table with a container of wine and departed. Commander Alban poured wine for both of them, then handed over the scroll. They both sat in silence as the centurion read the scroll.

Looking up from the scroll, Marcus looked to the commander and asked in an incredulous voice, "Is this order real? 'Immediate withdrawal of all troops and families as soon as this letter is received.'"

The commander cut some cheese up and took a bit. "Looks real enough, it's Emperor Honorius's seal."

Marcus looked at the scroll again. "Is this meant to be permanent?"

"I'm not sure," the commander replied. "But I am not surprised to receive this message. This problem with Alaric and his Vandals has been brewing for some time now but no one wants to admit it. Rome is in a mess and the Emperor has moved the senate to Ravenna. We must accept that this is real and start a pull out to the south and cross over to Gaul." The commander threw back some wine. "Wake up everyone, soldiers and families, and make sure they keep quiet. If those on the other side of this wall know what we are about to do, they may well attack."

"What about the wives and children?" Marcus asked.

"They'll be safe with us; we'll travel together with all five thousand soldiers, and more will join us in Gaul," the commander replied. Commander Alban stopped talking and quickly wrote up new orders, dropped wax on the papers and sealed them with his ring.

The servant, along with the rider, came back into the room. The commander handed one copy to the rider and one to the servant. Commander Alban looked at the servant. "Find another rider quickly, give him these orders, and tell him to ride to the western fort commander and give it to him. Go now." The servant turned and left in haste. The commander looked at the rider. "Give this message to the eastern fort commander. Do it now and stop for no one, understand?"

"Yes, Commander!" The messenger snapped a salute and left the room.

Alban looked at Marcus. "The western wall troops can meet us in Londinium."

"With these recent attacks on our defenses," Marcus replied, "it's possible the Picts are planning something. How do we protect our back, after we pull out and what about the slaves?"

"Slaves?" The commander replied, his mind far off. "Take only personal slaves and set the rest free. They will only burden us. As far as protecting our backs… Let me think about that. For now, get everyone up and ready to leave before dawn. Take no more than they can carry and bury the left-over possessions."

"Right," Marcus replied as he got up to leave. "Well, this should be interesting!"

The commander got up and went over to a rack of scrolls and put a few on his desk then dumped the rest on the floor. His wife, Julia, woke up from the noise he was making, got up and walked into his office.

"What is it?" she asked. "What's happening?

Her husband continued sorting out scrolls, with his back to her. "We have orders to evacuate Britannia and make haste to Rome. Best get up. Take only what you really need."

"What about the silver, cups, plates and my clothes?!"she asked.

"Bury what you cannot carry. We'll be back and collect it later, I'm sure," he snapped.

She looked at him as though he'd lost his mind. "Bury it! All of it!?"she asked in surprise.

The commander finally turned around. "Get on with it, we have to leave before sun-up and wake your daughter, Cassia, up," he called out.

His wife turned to leave. “Well, you were sent here because of your incompetence. Now they want you back. How fortunate. You can now see your high-class mistress again.”

Her husband threw some scrolls on the floor. “You talk too much. Get ready!” He then called out to the servant.

The servant came back into the room. “Yes, sir?”

The commander pointed to the floor. “Don’t waste any time, burn these scrolls in the courtyard, then help my wife.”

The servant started picking up the scrolls. The commander’s wife hastily walked from one room to another, frantically packing things needed for the trip.

***

The soldiers’ quarters covered ten buildings, with individual rooms of six men in each room. The centurion woke up a few of the soldiers in the barracks, hastily, stating, “Get up quietly, wake the rest, get dressed and pack all your gear, you have one hour.” He then headed to another barrack. The soldiers scratched their heads, rubbed the sleep from their eyes, and followed orders, wondering aloud if this was an early morning practice for a fight.

***

One hour later, the fifteen hundred men and family members lined up outside. Torches burned near the corners of the compound. A soldier dropped his shield and got the “evil eye” from his leader. Some soldiers came from the married quarters with sleepy children, babies with mothers, and all that they could carry. They all lined up behind the soldiers.

The commander came out, stood on a box, and addressed all the soldiers and families. "We have received orders to evacuate," he began, "to Londinium, then to Rome…immediately. No further explanation will be given until we reach Londinium. It's likely we will not be coming back soon."

A soldier called out from near the commander, "Are we going to be attacked?"

"Not here—no," the commander replied, "but Rome is. Now get ready to leave." With that, he got off the podium and left for his office. There was a general hum of concerned conversation. Some children started to cry, but the mother's hushed them up.

Wagons were loaded with food, weapons, and family members and lined up, ready for the gates to be opened. Centurion Marcus came over to Commander Alban's office. The commander, who was surveying the messy state of his office, looked up. "Did you do it?" he asked.

"Yes, it's all ready," the centurion replied.

"Then let's go before the cat is out of the bag," the commander replied, as they turned and left the office.

Centurion Marcus turned to the families and soldiers and gave the order to leave. "Open the gates!" Marcus called out. With that command the gates opened. Commander Alban and the rest of the army started to file out in marching form. False dawn reared its head.

The main gate opened to the outside road. The entire mass marched through the gates. Women and children sat on horse-drawn carts. Outside the gates sat a small collection of huts, owned by local traders. The line of soldiers moved slowly past the village, then stopped to let the families catch up. As they stopped, a small boy escaped from his mother's grip. Nearby, a tall, blond-haired young man moved forward to stop the boy. The boy complained, "Let me go!"

Letting the boy go back to his mother, he asked the mother, indicating the long line of people, "What's going on?"

"I don't know," the mother replied. "We were told to pack and that we may not come back. That's all I know."

"Not come back?" he asked. "Where are you all going?"

With some trepidation in her voice, she replied, "Londinium." The line started to move forward. "That's all I know." She called out, "Sorry, we have to leave now!" She got back into the line with her child. The line moved forward with half the troops in the front of the families and half in the back.

The tall, blond man stood to one side, and with one hand, counted the number of soldiers as they went by and added them to the beads he carried in his hand. He watched them all leave, then slowly followed the departing Romans all the way south.

***

Two days after the Romans left, on the north side of the wall, blue-faced, half-naked, armed men waited in the woods and watched the guards on the wall. There was no moon this night, but the fires lit by the wall guards lit up the wall somewhat. Old Chieftain Tyree, his advisor, Kesha, and a Druid priest also watched the wall guards.

Kesha sneered, "They've been here so long, that they have become lazy. Look how they stand, sleeping. Tyree, can we attack? The men are getting restless."

Chieftain Tyree stamped his staff and turned to his men. "Yes, give the signal."

Kesha silently lifted his arm up and waved a signal to the other men. Hundreds of men stood up and ran towards the wall, ready to fight, ready for spears and arrows—but none came.

They hit the wall, threw up ropes, and quickly scaled the wall, attacking the guards who put up the mildest of resistance and fell at the first hit. It quickly dawned on the Picts that all is not what it seemed.

Kesha, holding up a "Roman guard" called out, "These are not real soldiers! These are slaves!" while pulling at the slave collar around the so-called guard's neck.

The Druid priest looked at Chieftain Tyree. "We have been fooled! Where are the real guards?" he demanded from the slave.

"They've all left," the slave sputtered out.

Chieftain Tyree looked at the slaves being held by his men, then called out, "To the barracks!"

The Picts jumped down from the wall and attacked the barracks. Inside the barracks compound there was no one to be found. They searched from one room to another and from one building to another. Looking at the chieftain, Kesha wondered out loud, "It's either a trap or something is wrong. These Romans have been here for nine grandfathers back. They would not *just leave.*"

Chieftain Tyree looked about. "Well, they have, and look—they also have destroyed much of their own goods. These smell of pestilence!"

A local, old man was dragged into the compound by some of the Pict warriors and thrown to the ground in front of the chieftain. Looking at the villager he asked, "Where have they gone and when?"

"They left two nights ago!" the old man stuttered. "In a great hurry and took almost nothing, sir."

"And what of their womenfolk and children?" the chieftain asked.

"They also went with the soldiers."

The Druid priest asked the old man, "Is anyone sick in this village?"

"Sick? What do you mean?" asked the old man.

"Sick…pestilence, old fool!" spat the priest.

"None that I know of…" replied the old man.

Looking at the chieftain, the priest whispered, "We had better leave. I fear strange omens here."

Chieftain Tyree called out to his men, "Carry what you want, we leave now!" His men scurried about, loading up as much as they could carry and left the fort via the wall's gates which were now open.

JUTLAND, VIKING VILLAGE

Viking Chief Bjarke sat between his two advisers, Gunar the Elder and Alva. They sat and listened to the tall, blond man, Oden, fresh from his trip to England. The old chief shifted in his seat. "Oden, you say that all the Romans have left the island?"

Oden, standing before them said firmly, "Yes Bjarke. All of them, and all their fighting equipment and families."

"To where do you think they went?" went on the old Chief.

"I saw them gather in Londinium," Oden replied. "There were huge crowds and much lamenting. They seemed to be afraid, and many had no idea as to why they were told to leave, but leave they did, for Gaul."

The old chief turned to his advisors, "What are your thoughts Gunar?"

Gunar looked at Oden, "Did you see dead…from pestilence?"

"None," Oden said. "I walked from the wall to the city and saw no sickness, on the way or in the great city."

The woman, Alva, spun a knife in her hand. "Were the soldiers in an orderly procession? How did they look?"

"Procession? Yes. They seemed…well, confused," Oden replied.

Chief Bjarke leaned back in his chair and stared at Oden, seemingly unsure of what he was hearing. "And you say that all…all of the soldiers and their leaders have left the island?"

"It seemed so," Oden said. "But for a small force near Londinium."

The Chief sat up straight and looked hard at Oden. "You have done well, Oden." Looking at his advisers, he said, "Now, what shall we do, if anything?"

Gunar spoke up quickly, "We should attack now. If the Romans have truly gone, now is the time to strike if—"

Adviser Alva, interjected, "But if there is pestilence, our men will get this evil and bring it home. We must wait. Anyway, we do not have the men now to take this prize and keep it."

"If I may speak?" Oden asked.

"Speak Oden," the chief said.

"We could go step by step, taking the northernmost islands and see what happens from there," Oden said.

The chief and his advisers stared at him, then looked at each other, not wanting to give too much credibility to Oden for his new idea. "Let us think on that," replied Chief Bjarke.

***

The road to Londinium was long and wet. The caravan of carts, horses with soldiers, and foot soldiers, were spread out over three kilometres with horsemen acting as rear guard. Again, camp was broken. Cooking utensils, tents, bedding, and children were loaded into the wagons. Commander Alban rode on horseback in front of the standard carrier, and behind him, drummers beating out the marching rhythm. No one spoke, there was an eerie silence attached to the marching men and caravan.

Few talked, and all who they passed wondered what could have happened to cause the entire Roman army to leave at once. Peasant men, women, and children out and getting ready for the days planting, stopped when they saw the multitude of soldiers pass by on the road, and were surprised.

The womenfolk whispered to each other, the men gathered in groups and the atmosphere was strained. The word spread like wildfire, with all wondering the same thing. The soldiers and wagons moved quickly as they travelled through the wheat fields of central Britannia. Then as a trumpet sounded from the front, the entire marching caravan stopped near some fields for a break. The women to the right of the road and the men to the left and relieved themselves.

In the center of the caravan of carts, was the commander's wife, Julia, who sat inside a wagon, fixing some clothing. Her child, Cassia, now sixteen years of age, sat pouting next to her. "Why do we have to move? I never make any friends if we keep moving all the time."

Her mother looked up from her sewing. "It's not ours to ask why. Your father is the commander and has his orders, and we must follow what he says and where he goes."

"But we left everything this time, even your dinner set and extra clothing, and mine! Why must we leave so?" persisted Cassia.

Julia threw the needle and thread to Cassia in frustration. "Here, do some fixing!" she said to her daughter, who declined to catch them.

"I'm not doing that!" Cassia pouted. She jumped up and hopped out of the wagon.

Her mother calling after her, stuck her head out of the wagon. "Come back in here!" A few soldiers nearby laughed.

"No!" Cassia called back as she walked back towards the end of the line, head down.

Further back in the line of wagons and soldiers, Felix, a young teenage boy of seventeen years, was riding a horse towards Cassia. Seeing her coming his way, he stopped his horse. "Are you not the commander's daughter?"

Cassia looked up. "What of it soldier?"

"I'm not a soldier…yet," Felix replied. "May I offer you a ride?"

"No, you may not!" she replied as she walked around his horse and kept going at a faster pace. Felix looked back and shrugged.

All troops and families had commandeered a farmer's field and made camp for the evening. Families and soldiers alike made supper. Felix sat with his parents and watched his mother, Porcia, make supper over a campfire. His father, Decimus, sat sharpening and cleaning his sword. Felix used his small knife to sharpen a stick, stopped and looked at his father. "Father, today I met Commander Alban's daughter."

Decimus, who had started to apply honey to the swords edge, spoke softly to his son, "Oh, is that right son?"

"Yes, she was walking the wrong way."

"As they often do," his father replied.

"I offered her a ride," Felix went on.

"And…" his father prodded.

"She became angry with me and…kept walking," Felix finished.

"Her father is from a good Roman family, Felix. We are not. She is above your station, best leave her alone son," his father admonished.

"She is quite…beautiful." Felix went on.

Decimus put down his sword. "Even worse. Seek after Betha. Her father is a metalsmith. She would make a fine wife, son."

"Betha?" replied Felix. "She is too short!"

Porcia pointed her ladle at her son. "She would make a good cook and a mother."

"I'm too young to marry and I'm not interested in Betha!" Felix snapped back. He got up and walked away in a huff.

Porcia looked at her husband. "The grape does not fall far from the vine."

Decimus, with a warning face, pointed his sword at her. "Don't start!"

***

Further into the center of the campsite was a large, grand tent. Inside, Commander Alban, his wife Julia, Centurion Marcus with his wife, Alva, and a few guests reclined on makeshift beds, drinking wine, eating, and chatting. Fires warmed the tent, with two servants serving food and drinks, while two guards were posted at the door outside. Julia popped raisins into her mouth and kept the discourse lively. "Do we have enough boats?"

Her husband looked at her carefully and sipped wine before answering, "Of course my dear. That, you do not have to worry about. There is no one chasing us. We have ships and food. It's time, we do not have."

Alva, wife of Marcus stabbed another piece of meat and put it onto her plate. "And what about the weather? The seas are so cold and rough."

Her husband, Marcus, spat out seeds onto the floor. "My love. The seas will be as they were when we came here two years ago. High seas or not, we leave."

"How many marching days to Rome?" Julia asked again. "And what about those bands of marauding Vandals? The sacked Durocortorum and Augustodunum?"

Commander Alban put down his wine. "The Vandals are long gone into Spain, so you need not worry. We have to move east first to Durocortorum city to collect supplies. Its has revived somewhat. There we will meet up with the army defending the Germanic wall. After that, it's all the way to Massalia on the coast, so maybe thirty days marching."

A female guest sat up and adjusted her robe against the chill of the night. "We will arrive into Londinium tomorrow. There will be questions from the locals. What shall we tell them, Marcus?"

Marcus looked down at his wine and reflected a moment. "We are not going directly into the city, but around it. If someone asks, tell them as the great Caesar said, 'We'll be back soon, ha!'" All attempted a weak laugh, but each had their own thoughts.

***

Eighteen days later the troops moved onto fields close to Londinium city. The entire column of soldiers, carts, wagons, and families formed a long line, and set camp near the city. They stopped at the market stalls to fill up on supplies.

Thousands of Romans from the south of Britannia, were already camped there with their families. The entire combined army looked like a tent city equal the size of Londinium. The commander Appius, of the southern troop command, rode up to meet Commander Alban. Appius saluted Alban. "Commander! South Command reporting! What are your orders?"

"We'll leave for the ships in a few hours," said Alban. "Please have your men ready."

"Of course," replied Appius. "I can hardly believe we are actually going through with this!"

Commander Alban moved closer to Appius. "I dare not voice what we will face in Italy."

"And what we will find when we come back here., said Appius.

"If we come back," Alban retorted. "But we took it once, we can always retake it."

Appius looked at Alban. "I suppose so."

Both men sat on their horses and stared out into the countryside and then the mass of tents. The city could be seen and as it woke up, smoke curled into the sky and blotted the morning sun as meals were prepared by the city folk and for ten thousand troops. More and more folk, especially the young, came to the markets to see the amazing sight of so many Romans on their way southeast. Other, richer families, coming from the city, who had been forewarned, joined the Romans, wagons packed with furniture, bedding and tents, with money either buried for use when they returned or safely tucked away in their wagons.

As the sun rose in the morning sky, councillors from the basilica and other local city fathers made their way to see Commander Alban who was talking to his men about food supplies. A councillor interrupted the commander by pushing his way through the soldiers. "Commander! Please! What is going on here? It looks like the entire army is leaving!"

Commander Alban swung around to face the councillors. "Ah, Councillor, it's just temporary. We are only providing protection to our families as they leave for Rome."

"But…but you seem to have everyone here. Who will protect us from marauding bands of Jutes, Saxons, or other heathens?"

"I can assure you," Commander Alban replied, "we will be right back. You need not worry about anything. We will leave some troops here, to protect you, with Aubrosuis Arthor in charge. He can help you form a…a…'people's army.'"

"But it's not only about soldiers. If you are leaving, we will lose income derived from the army! Our businesses will collapse and who will collect the taxes?"

Commander Alban loosened the white cloth around his neck as his frustration started to show. "We will be back, and you councillors will be leaving soon yourselves. Now, please get out of the way, we have to pack up these supplies and make the coast today. The tides and wind wait for no one." The commander moved forward with his men.

The town council huddled together chatting and complaining while wringing their hands in nervousness. The councillors looking fearfully at the Roman commander and troops, while uttering over and over again, "May Jupiter protect us all!"

The Romans, both families and soldiers, walked the nearby food stalls choosing what limited food they could take on the ships. Felix saw Cassia and walked up behind her as she picked out some apples. "So much to choose from," he said.

Cassia turned to see who was talking to her. Momentarily forgetting her previous encounter with him as she placed the apples in her basket. "Oh! Yes! So much. I'm not sure what to take!"

Felix took her basket. "Here, let me carry that. My father said to eat nothing before getting on the ship or you will get seasick."

Cassia let him take her basket as they walked back to the camp. "Oh, really? What ship are you on?"

"We are on number fifty-six, and you?" he replied.

"Number one."

"Oh, I see. Well, I'll see you on the other side."

She took her basket from him, and looked him over from bottom to top. "Maybe," she replied with half a smile. She then turned and left him.

***

In the distance the army trumpets sounded to let all know that the march was on again. The troops and families started again down the road towards the coastal port. Hundreds of ships lined the coast or were busy coming and going from the port. The troops, horses, and families boarded the ships. As soon as they were full, they set sail. The seas looked calm, but a strong wind pushed the sails towards the opposite coastline.

Many men, women, and children, got seasick, spending the entire trip with their heads hanging over the sides vomiting into the green seas. The ships docked on the Gaul side, with soldiers debarking first. The family wagons and armaments were the last off. Everyone lined up again and headed down the road, eastward. No one talked; all were tired or still recovering from the sea trip. The entire army and wagons with families headed further and further eastward down the road as they headed for Durocortorum where they would resupply with food.

Local Gaelic peasants lined the road here and there, wondering at the sheer number of the army and where they were off to. On one side stood Egono from the northern tribes, a tall, dark-faced man, with long, braided hair and pocked face, watching the procession head eastward. He counted the number of men, by making knots in a rope for each fifty that passed by. The line finally finishing, he turned north and left .

The entire army and their families took over wheat fields, trampling down the wheat without a care as they made one camp after another. Midway to Durocortorum, already two hundred kilometres covered, the camp woke up and thousands of them headed to the nearby river to wash, and then dress and eat; the men over to one side and the women and children on the other.

When the trumpet sounded, the soldiers lined up and started marching with a thousand horsemen leading the way. The families then came behind the soldiers. More soldiers fell in behind the families and another thousand horsemen behind them.

***

That evening in the commander's tent, Commander Alban, Centurion Marcus, and other centurions looked over a map of Gaul. Commander Alban pointed to the west on the map. "We have five thousand men joining us later today from the western Germanic wall," pointing to the eastern wooden wall, he continued, "then another five thousand from the eastern Germanic wall. All these men, plus the south Britannia army will leave us at the Chalon River and head south by boat as fast as they can to Rome. The rest will protect the families and go by road. Questions?"

Sub Commander Appius looked carefully at the map. "Once the Germanic Wall is undefended, how long will it take before the Germanic tribes understand what is going on?"

Alban smiled. "Worried about an attack? The families will have five thousand men with them. One thousand will be on horseback. We have the finest army in the world. We can take care of any problems. Any other questions?"

Another commander piped up, "Marching time to Massilia?"

"From here to the eastern Germanic wall and Durocortorum, about ten days and south to Massilia, about twenty days, weather permitting," Alban replied.

And yet another commander asked, "Any news from Rome?"

"Hopefully we will get some news in Massilia. Any other questions?" Alban said. None were raised. Commander Alban rolled up the map. "Then let's get going." They all departed the tent.

***

The next day, five thousand troops from the western wall marched from the north, met the Commander, and joined the march east. The wagons and armies stretched over eight kilometres, moved eastward towards the Chalon River and the town Marville, a trading center. More and more forest land and less open fields greeted them, but the road east was well worn. The immense army once again camped in open fields for the night.

Decimus stood near his wagon along with another man. "Felix! Come over here!" he called out. Felix came over from the field with two buckets of water for his mother. He dropped them near his mother who sat making supper over a fire. Decimus pointed the man next to him. "Felix, this is Sabini. He is a Travini veteran from the Germanic wall." They gripped each other's arms in greetings. Decimus continued, "He will be with us until the river. I have asked him to train you, as you will soon join the Hastati front fighting ranks. You need to be prepared."

Felix looked at his father. "But I want to—"

"Never mind what you want!" Decimus interjected. "If you are to follow me, you must be prepared to join the Hastati. As we move along Sabini will be training you, understand?"

"Yes father," Felix replied.

Sabini gave Felix a slap on the shoulder in a fatherly way. "Worry not, boy, we have lots of time to get you into fighting shape," Sabini said, smiling. Felix gave a weak smile back. Both men laughed and sat down to eat while his mother served them.

***

Over the next week, the long line of wagons and troops continued to move eastward at a steady pace. The sun rose and set with the army making and breaking camp each time. Each evening, Sabini took Felix outside the camp and into the nearby woods and trained him how to defend himself using a shield, a short sword for close-up kills, and to use the javelin. As days went by, Felix improved.

Sabini stood in an open area with a sword, watching Felix on horseback, working the horse to and fro as Felix attacked Sabini. Nearby, hidden behind a tree, sat Cassia, watching Felix as he trained. She bit her lip and twirled her hair on one side as she watched him practice. After a while, she got up and headed towards her tent where her mother was and entered the tent. Her mother Julia sat eating her supper with one dish opposite her, still empty.

"Well, are you going to eat?"

"Yes," Cassia said curtly. A servant girl came over and gave her a bowl of soup and a cup, and then poured some wine.

Her mother watched her eat. "Where do you go each afternoon, Cassia?"

"Just walking," Cassia replied.

"You be careful, there are ten thousand men outside this tent. You understand?"

"They know who I am," replied Cassia, "and who my father is."

"You just be careful," her mother voiced again.

Cassia changed the subject, "Some say we are refugees. Is that true? Are we refugees now?"

Her mother laughed. "Of course not! We are simply returning to Rome."

"But why so suddenly and why so many?" Cassia pressed. "Men from all the frontiers' walls? Today father says the eastern army joined us."

Julia stood up. “Ours is not to ask why. These are dangerous times and changes are upon us, and you, my daughter had better be prepared.”

Cassia stood up. “Prepared for what?”

“Cassia,” her mother replied in frustration, “you are a such a child! Anything you desire can be had. But the Gods can be fickle. What we have now can be taken away at a moment’s notice!”

“Are you trying to scare me?” Cassia asked, eyeing her mother.

“Yes, I am,” her mother replied. “Rome is under threat from northern heathens. Even in Rome, our lives are at the mercy of the army and Emperors and many of them are not fit to wear the purple. The future is most uncertain.”

“And cooking, sewing, and bearing children will save me?” Cassia spat out sarcastically.

Julia picked up some clothing, replying gruffly, “A good Roman wife can do that and more.”

Cassia stamped her foot. “I’m not going to marry!”

“Bearing children when you are young is the best way!” her mother snapped back.

“All you want is grandchildren! I’m getting cold and going to bed!” Cassie replied as she turned to leave.

Julia picked up a short pole and was about to use it on Cassia. Cassia, seeing what her mother was about do, picked up another pole. They both started fighting, using the poles as swords, falling over furniture as her mother berated her. The servant looked on in shock.

Julia struck Cassia. "I am told you are talking with that boy again!"

"Who told you that?" Cassia screamed out as she hit her mother's pole. Sticks crashed against each other again and again.

"You are forbidden to see that boy, or any other! I have someone chosen for you in Rome!" her mother screamed out.

Cassia hit her mother's pole again and again. "I am…not…going to…marry…someone you…choose for me!" she puffed out.

Suddenly the tent flaps opened, and the commander stepped into the tent. "Am I missing something!?" he asked, somewhat in humor.

Both women dropped their sticks. "Your child is not listening to me!" his wife shouted to him.

Cassia's father winked at Cassia. "Listen to your mother. In less than week we will reach Durocortorum and you two can take a break from each other." Cassia gave a dismissive sniff and walked over to her bed.

Julia walked to her husband. "She's just like you—stubborn!"

The next morning as the army moved eastward, Cassia stopped her mother's servant, and confronted her. "You've been spying on me!" Cassia accused.

The servant girl dropped her head. "Mistress, your mother ordered me to!"

"Well, I'm ordering you not to!" Cassia replied, as she handed her some coins. "If she asks, tell her I'm visiting other girls, understand?"

"Yes, mistress," the servant replied as she eyed the coins in her hand. They went their separate ways.

***

Every late afternoon when they stopped to make camp, Sabini took Felix into the nearest woods to practice. Felix stood watching Sabini handle the shield. "Felix. There are three stances with the shield," Sabini said. "First shoulder height, second, on the ground to defend, and third, the "turtle" to use with other men." He showed Felix and then Felix tried, up and down quick movements until Felix's shoulders ached from holding the heavy shield.

Felix and Sabini wrapped up their training. Sabini left Felix and returned to the camp for supper. Felix stayed behind, as usual, and cleaned his sword, wiped down his horse, then collected his armaments. From behind a tree, Cassia stepped out and walked up to him. She stared down at him as he knelt to pick up his sword.

Felix, seeing her feet looked up. "What?" he asked.

"I want you to teach me to use a sword," she ordered.

Felix opened his mouth in surprise. "What! But your a…a—"

"What? A woman? I can fight too!" she said in a haughty voice.

"But... Why?" he asked.

Cassia looked about, rather embarrassed more than anything, but trying not to show it. "Why? Just because I'm a girl does not mean I can't fight. I can fight! Show me how."

Felix hesitated. "What will you do for me?"

"I don't have much money," she replied.

"Ah, well—" Felix said, trying to help her out.

Cassia butted in, "I can teach you Latin!"

"Why do I need Latin?" he asked in surprise.

"Rome does not speak Celtic, Felix!"

"Oh," he replied.

"So…do you agree?" she asked.

Felix looked at her, then shook his head and handed her one of two swords. "Let's start then." He gave her a leather chest protector which she put it on. "You've got that on the wrong way round," Felix admonished. She took it off as he helped her put it on the right way. Cassia held the sword.

"This wooden sword is so heavy!" she commented, swing it wildly left and right.

"Yes, it's called a practice gladius for practicing fighting," Felix said, trying to copy Sabini's authoritative tone of voice. He showed her how to stand, to hold the sword correctly, how to thrust, and where to aim the hit. He struck out at her time and time again, hitting her sides and front until she dropped the sword. He backed up and picked it up for her and gave it back. "There are two places to use the sword," he said as he showed her where to hit the opponent by hitting a wooden pole.

Felix struck the pole from the top of the shield or from the side. They continued. He corrected her as they moved about, calling out to her, "Hold the gladius tighter! Keep your legs apart! Keep your body sideways and move faster!" Finally, she dropped the sword and dropped to the ground exhausted.

Felix moved over to where she sat. "It will take time." She looked up at him as he extended his hand to help her up. "We will train again tomorrow," he concluded.

She brushed herself off then abruptly left, calling out, "And your first Latin lesson afterwards!" She walked off out of the woods without a look back.

***

Later that evening, Felix's family sat in their tent eating supper. Decimus shoved stew into his mouth, swallowed and said, "Sabini tells me you are improving quickly."

Between bites, Felix looked up from his bowl. "Oh…yes? Thank you."

"Maybe you should join the troops in the boats going south?" his father went on.

"Oh?! No, no! I need more time to practice!" Felix blurted out.

"I see," said his father. "Well keep up the good work, time will come when you need it." Felix stuck his face into his food, as the father and mother eyed him carefully.

***

The caravan of wagons and soldiers finally reached their eastern destination of Durocortorum. It was an old, established trading post facing the Germanic tribes to the east and with a wooden wall facing the north that kept out marauding bands of Saxons and Anglos. The troops and caravan of wagons marched into a field near the town, and set up camp once again. The troops sat about resting and cleaning their equipment. A guard was put in around the camp area and a general sigh of relief came from most, as they released that it was downhill from here on and most would take to the river to move southward.

The commander's tent was full of men listening as Commander Alban addressed them. He looked up from the maps, and said, "We will rest here in for two days. Gather food and wine. The troops from the Germanic border with most of my men from Britannia, will head for the Chalon River, they are needed in Rome as soon as possible."

Marcus looked down at the map. "Are you still counting on three weeks to Massalia?"

"Given good weather, yes. We will have all the families but also two cohorts to protect them. It should be enough. There's been no problems in this area for some time." He then looked at Marcus. "Marcus. Give the orders to the troops going on the boats to pack up. Appius, you are to command them." Marcus and the others salutee and left the tent.

***

The next morning found Cassia and Felix sitting next to an aqueduct with a small river running under it. Cassia tapped the dirt with a stick. "Just repeat after me, it's not so hard. Gratias tibi"

Felix tried to copy her. "Gracies tidi."

"Grat-ias TI-BI," she corrected.

Felix corrected himself, “Grat…ias…tibi”

“Right,” she said. “Gratias tibi”

“What’s that mean?” he asked.

“It means thank you. Next one. Goodbye is vale!”

“Vale! That was easy,” he said.

“Next,” she went on, “good morning is bonum mane.”

Felix repeated, “Bonum man.”

“No! Pay attention,” she admonished. “Bonum mane!”

“Bonum mane,” he repeated with a sour look.

“What was the first one?” she demanded.

“The first? Grat tibi?” he guessed.

“Really Felix! Gratias tibi. I think I will better with the sword compared to your Latin ability!” She laughed. “One more. Yes please is etiam commodo,” she commanded.

“Eww…etamu commando?” Felix spat out as he tried to copy her accent. Cassia rolled over laughing.

Felix stood up, frustrated. “Alright, alright. Write them down and I will practice!”

“Ha! Can you read?” she laughed.

“My reading is better than your swordsmanship!” he shot back as he picked up the reading slate and gave it to her.

“I will write down those three and test you tomorrow,” she replied as she did so. Then finished, they both got up and left the riverside, walking a bit closer together as they did so.

On the cliff above where they sat a group of Germanic men and one woman, sat on their horses, swords and bows clasped to their backs, watching the goings-on between Felix and Cassia. Egono looked at the others. "What I told you is right. They came from the ships and now Durocortorum and they will all head south. The Romans look like they are all going home and look at their women," he said as he pointed. "I will take that one," pointing down to Cassia. They laughed quietly.

Adelbern the elder smiled. "Maybe you will, but you might have to wait till I have her."

Badurad, the young female pointed to Cassia. "We can take them all now!"

Adelbern looked about. "No. We wait. See what they do with all those boats on the river. If they do leave, we can take what we want from what they leave behind."

Egono the younger looked disappointed. "So, we do not attack? If they all use the boats, we will have nothing."

Adelbern turned his horse about and muttered, "Egono, learn to wait. There are too few boats for all of them. Wait a bit longer." They turned their horses and silently rode back into the forest.

***

The Durocortorum town councillor, his council, along with Commander Alban and Marcus, sat in the town leader's house. Scowls on one and tired eyes on the other. basilica councillor spoke Gaelic through a translator to the commander. "Are you serious? We have supplies to give to you but that is not the question. We have been here, servicing you and your army since you came here hundreds of years ago, and now you're telling me that you and all these people are leaving but will be back soon! Is this that I will tell the town people?" the translator relayed to the commander.

"Yes," the commander replied via the translator. "It's what you will tell them. I'll leave some troops with you until we get back. The tribes here and in the north have been quiet and cooperative. There is nothing to fear."

"Nothing to fear. And if you do not return, should we fear?" replied the councillor.

"I have my orders," said the commander. "Rome is under attack from Vandals, and we are in need. Now, if you don't mind, we have much to prepare." And with that comment, he and Marcus drank the last of their offered wine and departed the house.

The town leader and his men look at each other in incredulous dismay and apprehension. The councillor threw up his hands, uttering, "May Apollo protect us all."

***

Later that day, the commander and his generals took a good look at the map of Gaul on the table, then Commander Alban addressed his men. "Tomorrow, most of the troops will depart by boats waiting on the Chalon River to south Gaul, then to Rome."

Marcus pondered over the order. “This town is not happy with ‘we’ll be back.’ Can we really leave them undefended?”

“I have decided to leave a contingent here. They will have to keep the peace. There is no reason to think we will not be coming back.”

A subcommander spoke up, “And the Belguis and Germanics?”

“They are not going to do anything. They know the consequences if they take matters into their own hands,” the commander replied.

“Let’s hope you are right,” said Marcus, to a room full of doubting faces.

“Alright,” commander said. “Let’s get the men and equipment into the boats.”

“We need some help loading up the boats,” said the third subcommander.

“Draw some from the guard details. We start tomorrow before dawn,” Alban stated in a firm voice as he rolled up the maps. The commanders saluted and left the tent.

“Right. I’ll see to it,” said Marcus and left with the rest.

***

At the crack of dawn, with the dew still wet on the ground, the camp was broken for most of the men. Thousands of Roman troops marched ten kilometres south with their equipment, to the river and lined up at the riverbank.

Three hundred boats waited for the soldiers. They loaded up the equipment and then the men boarded the boats. Swords sheathed, their kits over their respective shoulders, one by one, the men entered the boats. They stowed their gear as best they could on the overloaded boats and manned the oars. The last in was the standard bearer and the Germanic wall commander. He turned before entering the lead boat, saluted the commander goodbye, and entered his boat. The Roman men on the shore helped push the barges off into the water. The barges and boats floated into midstream and headed south. The commander and the rest of his men stood down before returning to the camp to eat a light breakfast from their rations.

The camp was silent as families and soldiers slept or were waking up. The guards along the camp parameters, instead of guarding, picked up the belongings scattered along the broad trail left by the troops, who were now nearing the ships ten kilometres away.

North of the camp, deep the forest, a fog hid the Germanic forces waiting on horseback for the command. Adelbern raised his hand, his men moved out of the woods at a trot, then nearer to the camp, charged out of the fog right into the arms of the surprised guards. Horses flew over or on top of the guards and into the camp. Guards dropped the gear they had been carrying and ran for the perimeter only to be cut down by horsemen. The riders entered the camp area, jumped off their horses to catch running women and jumped skillfully back onto their horses, taking off back through the guards who were now headed into the camp.

Felix and his father sat up from their beds. Hearing the commotion Decimus called out to his son, “Felix! Quickly get your sword and follow me!”

Felix, without a word scrambled out of his bed, grabbed his sword, and followed his father out of the tent. Outside, mayhem ensued. Decimus cut down the nearest German to come past him on horseback. Felix followed him, stabbing the fallen Germanic has he lay dying. Decimus slashed out at other passing horsemen, screaming out orders to nearby confused Romans. “Get the horses! Get your ass into it!” The Romans, now getting organized, started to chase the Germanics back into the forest.

Egono the Germanic rode for a large tent just as Julia stepped out of the tent with her servant. Egono seeing Julia, rode up to her, punched her in the head, knocking her senseless. As she fell, he jumped off his horse, grabbed her and slung her over his horse and rode off around the tent and into the woods. Her servant ran back into the tent, just as Cassia was about to come out, she pushed Cassia to the back with Cassia complaining the whole way, then she turned and ran out of the tent, frying pan in hand, only to be hit by Albertson’s horse.

Alberton grabbed her by the hair, pulled her up on onto his horse and fled into the fields and woods. Hearing the commotion outside, Cassia grabbed a knife then fled towards the back door of the tent. She moved out the door, right into the arms of Felix, almost sticking him with her knife. “They attacked my tent!” she gasped.

Felix held her knife hand away from his stomach. "Are you alright!?" he asked.

"Yes," she replied, catching her breath. "But I'm not sure of my servant or my mother! Let me fight!"

Decimus came up behind them, and overheard what she said. "No. Women don't fight."

"I can fight! Felix has been training me!" she blurted out without thinking.

"What?!" Decimus asked gruffly as he wiped the blood from his blade.

"I was only showing her how—" Felix jumped in before being interrupted by a soldier.

"Decimus! We are needed at the north perimeter!" Felix's father moved away, shouting back to Felix, "We'll talk later. Help get the horses rounded up!"

Cassia looked at Felix. "I've made trouble for you."

"Never mind," he replied. "Help me get the horses."

As fast as it started it was over. Bodies of guards lay here and there with some of the Germanics. Horses ran about without riders. Felix with Cassia help round them up. Families came out of tents, casting fearful looks left and right. The fog had lifted, the sun shone down on the dead, and the Germanics, with their captive women, fled into the deep forests.

At the river, Commander Alban, Centurion Marcus, and their men, turned their horses back north towards their camp, only to find the camp in total disarray with soldiers burning the dead and counting the missing horses and women. Commander Alban came into his tent to find Marcus waiting there. “What in Jupiter’s name happened here and where are my centurions?” Alban demanded.

Marcus, who was standing near the table, sat down. “The Germanics did not wait long and have obviously been trailing us. And as for the centurions, they will arrive soon. I need to talk to you first though.”

“About what?” Alban demanded.

“You had better sit down.” Marcus stated.

The commander gives him a quizzical look but sat down. “I’m sorry to report that your wife was captured by the Germanics,” Marcus said softly.

The commander clutched his chest. “What?”

“It has been reported that your wife has been taken captive,” Marcus replied softly.

“Jupiter’s wrath!” replied Alban. “Do we do have time to pursue them if we dispatch troops now?”

“Yes, we could…” started Marcus.

Two subcommanders came into the tent, they all saluted Alban. “Commander. What are your orders?”

Alban stood up. "You are to take one hundred mounted men," Alban began, "and pursue those Germanics. Leave now and keep your eyes out for captured women."

Subcommander looked perplexed. "Anyone in particular?"

"My wife," the commander replied.

The men look at him, stunned into silence. "We will leave now!" the subcommander replied and left with the others. Soon after, the mounted Roman troops entered into the forest following the tracks of the Germanics.

Now angry, Alban sat down. "Put the word out Marcus, we leave at dawn."

"Yes sir. But your wife?" replied Marcus.

"We have our orders. The search party will find her and can catch up to us." Alba stood up again, then, remembering his daughter he looked around. "Where is my daughter?"

"I saw her as I came this way. I'll send someone to find her," Marcus replied. They both sat down again. Alban poured wine for them. They both sat there in silence, pondering the consequences of today's attack.

By evening guards were back on duty, and the camp defenses were repaired. The camp was quiet as the families and soldiers sat about eating. Decimus and his family sat and ate. "You did well today," Felix's father said, "but what did that girl mean? Was that not the commander's daughter?"

The mother, Porcia looked up from her bowl. Felix started to eat faster. "She wanted to ride a horse; I was just showing her."

Porcia added more soup to Decimus's bowl. "She will bring only trouble my son. Be careful what you do."

Decimus looked carefully at his son. "Stick to your lessons my boy," he said. Felix kept his head down, nodded his agreement and ate faster.

***

The following day, troops were ready; some were on guard duty and the rest getting ready to leave. In the commander's tent, Marcus awaited his orders. Commander Alban looked at the map on the table while his daughter sat nearby. He looked up at Marcus. "Give the order to break camp."

Marcus gave a snappy salute. "Yes Commander," he replied and departed.

The commander turned to his daughter. "Cassia. Until your mother is returned, you will have to take care of cooking, cleaning, and such."

Cassia looked up in surprise. "But I can't cook and clean. That's servant's work!"

"Cassia," her father replied, "may I remind you that we have no servants anymore, so you had better start learning and you can start now."

"But…but…"she sputtered.

"No buts, get the wagon loaded now," her father ordered.

"Just me?" she asked.

Over his shoulder he replied as he walked out the tent door, "just you...will be good practice for when you marry!"

The wagons and soldiers move southward towards Massilia, with more haste in their footsteps, as if trying to outrun the problems and raids that had plagued the north. The south was safer, warmer, and closer to fresh fish, fruit, and Italy. Commander Alban rode up to his own wagon where Cassia sat in the front with a soldier driver. "What have you decided for our supper?" he asked Cassia.

"Er...rabbit stew, Father," she called from the seat.

"Rabbit? From where?" he asked.

"A friend," she replied carefully.

"Good friend," he replied. "I'll see you at sunset." And with that he rode off to the front of the marching soldiers.

As soon as he was gone, Cassia raced back to where Felix's wagon was moving along and jumped aboard the wagon's front seat next to Felix's surprised mother. "I need your help!" she said to the surprised woman.

"What... But you are..." replied Porcia.

"Yes I know! But I need your help now! I need to cook for my father!" she demanded.

"But why me? You have a servant," Porcia replied.

"No. My mother and servant were carried off by the Germanics," Cassia replied sadly.

"Ah, I see. What can I do for you?" Felix's mother asked.

"I need to cook a rabbit stew for my father tonight."

"And?" asked Porcia.

"And… I will pay you to teach me," said Cassia a bit more humbly.

"Alright," said Porcia. "But not in salt! My husband has enough of his pay in salt. Coin only."

"I have my mother's money. I will pay you well enough in coin. Can we start now?" replied Cassia, getting frustrated.

"Yes, as soon as we stop," said Porcia.

"And one more thing," Cassia added.

"What's that?" asked Porcia.

"Don't tell Felix or my father," said Cassia.

"I won't be telling anyone including my husband or Felix," replied Porcia.

***

Felix and Cassia continued to meet in the forest. Soldiers watching them enter the woods, chuckled as to what they thought was going on. Felix stood in a clearing in the woods impatiently waiting for Cassia. "Where have you been?" he demanded.

"Taking care of my father," she replied as Felix handed her armor and a spear.

"Sabini has been showing me some spear techniques. This is your catafracta and pilum, your armor and spear. I will show you," Felix said.

They faced off. Felix started to instruct her. "Keep moving around." They circled about. "Keep the opponent away from you and keep your body low." They continued to practice. Finally they stopped.

Cassia took off her armor and sat on the ground sweating, then reached into her bag. "I wrote your lessons on this tablet." She passed the tablet to him. He frowned as he studied it for a few minutes. Cassia pulled the tablet from him. "Can you remember? What is thank you?"

"Gratias tibi," he replied.

"And goodbye?"

"Vale," he replied quickly.

"And would you like?" she asked.

"Did we study that one?" Felix asked.

"It's today's lesson. Would you like is velis," she said.

"Velis? Is that it? Just one word?" he replied.

"Yes," she said. "The next phrase. Yes please is etiam commodo. Remember that one?" she asked.

"No," he replied. "But I do know another one."

"Oh?" she said.

Felix moved towards her face, eyes closed, and lips pursed. "Ut ego te basia?"

She got up quickly. "Kiss you! Your Latin is getting sooo good!" She turned her face from him. He stood up blushing. She picked up her spear and turned towards him and challenged him with the spear. Felix grabbed a shield. "You forget your place!" she called out.

Felix fended off her attack. “And what is my place!?” he called out as he backed up.

Cassia faked a charge at him then suddenly dropped the spear and walked away, calling over her shoulder as she left, “It’s late. I must tend to my father’s needs. Practice the Latin I taught you!” as she disappeared into the woods and camp.

***

The commander sat behind a portable table. The officers who had chased after the tribesmen, entered the tent and saluted. Cassia stood at the back of the tent preparing supper. The centurion commanders stepped forward. “I am sorry to report that we could not find the raiding party…or your wife.”

Alban stared at them as he comprehended the meaning. “I see. May Juno protect her.”

“We will give sacrifice tonight,” offered the centurion.

“Thank you. We will do that and also double the guard. Keep your men alert, we have about fifteen days marching before we get to Massilia. Stay alert.”

The men saluted and left. Alban turned around. “Cassia, bring me that stew.” She got up, went to a table and brought it over to him. He tasted the stew. “Mmm good. You heard what the centurion said?”

She looked at her the stew, and as tears ran down her face she dropped her spoon. “We were always fighting with each other,” she whispered, through the tears.

"They will not kill her," Alban said, "but they will use her for labor. We will find her. Worry not. We will find her." He got up and came over to her, opened his arms and held her.

She folded herself into her father's arms as she cried. "I…just…want…her back." Her father looked off, wondering other things, like what his mistress would say.

***

The road south was worn out with travel over hundreds of years, but was still in better condition than the north. The soldiers marched onward, feeling the temperature rise which in turn made their armor hotter to wear, but with the recent attacks there was no option. Bets were made as to who would smell the Mediterranean Sea first. The wagons followed them, kicking up the dust so that those in the back wagons ate dust all day long. This time there were more mounted men along the route and in nearby fields watching out for attacks.

Porcia sat inside her wagon with Cassia showing her how to sew. It had lately dawned on Cassia that in addition to looking after the cooking and cleaning, she would also have to see to her father's tent, repairs, and clothing. Porcia pointed to the needle. "Look where the needle has entered the cloth, then carefully enter back as close as possible to the last point."

Cassia tried sewing with a pair of her father's pants. "I never thought I would be asked to sew my father's pants," she commented, half to herself.

Porcia watched her with an eagle's eye. "A woman's place is not behind her husband but beside him. But if you want to keep that position, you need to understand how fixing your future husband's pants will help you as a woman."

Cassia stopped sewing, replying gruffly, "I am not seeking a husband."

Porcia pointed towards the needle. "Be careful with that needle. No, you may not be seeking, but he may be seeking you."

"I'm just fixing my father's pants!" Cassia replied, somewhat miffed.

"Fixing pants is one way to see what's in it," Porcia laughed.

"What?!" Cassia replied shocked at her comment. "What do you mean?"

Porcia smiled at her. "You'll soon find out. Here, let me finish that, it will take you all day."

Cassia handed her the pants along with the needle and thread. "I'll pay you today." Cassia offered. She handed some coins to Porcia who looks at them carefully. "I must leave," Cassia said, getting up.

"Don't forget the raisins," Porcia said as she passed a bag to Cassia. Cassia thanked her jumped out of the moving wagon and walked back to her wagon.

***

Felix worked out daily with Sabini, working on his horsemanship and learning to fight from the horse. Felix sat on his horse with a sword in one hand. Sabini on the ground nearby, pointed to the horse. "Hold the horse with your thighs and strike down with your gladius, left and right to the enemy's head and shoulders. Felix did so and hitting down at Sabini who ducked skillfully out of the way each time. Felix attacked again but lost his balance and fell off the horse. He picked himself up and dusted his tunic off.

Sabini looked at Felix. "You can hold the reins with your left hand. Try again and grip the horse well with your thighs!" Felix tried again and again, each time getting up and back onto the horse, doing better each time.

Finally, Sabini called Felix to dismount. "You're catching on. Let's look at your shield." Felix dismounted, let the horse feed off the grass and walked over towards Sabini with his shield in hand. Sabini took hold of Felix's shield. "The shield," Sabini said as he demonstrated, "can be used to protect your body and you have nothing to worry about if your men are to the sides of you but take care if you are alone. Use the shield if you need, to strike the enemy. Attack me now!"

He demonstrated by attacking then defending from with a shield as Felix attacked him. Decimus came over to them and watched Felix practice with the shield. "Very good son!" he called out. Sabini and Felix turned towards the voice. "Thank you, Sabini, for teaching my son. He's coming along well," he complimented.

"He'll do alright, just needs to add some weight and muscle to him."

Decimus turned to leave. “Let’s eat.”

“Father, please start without me. I’m going to feed and clean the horse, I’ll be along soon.”

“Alright son,” his father called back.

Sabini turned to leave. “Remember what I said about cleaning your sword. To protect it from rust, warm the blade. Warmer than body heat but not to so warm as to ruin the blade, and then polish beeswax in it. It makes the blade have a dull shine but protects it from rusting.” And with that, his father and Sabini left.

Felix cleaned his sword, shield, and sarcina then fed his horse. It was late and the sun was now on the horizon. Cassia came out of the bushes. “You’re late, let’s start before it gets dark.” Felix said.

Cassia, unsmiling, replied with a quiet, “Alright.” She picked up a sword and started to work out with him but her spirit was not into it.

Felix stopped and looked at her. “Are you alright?”

She put the sword down and dropped her head and whispered, “She is not coming back to me.”

Felix stopped and looked at her. “Oh… I heard. I’m sorry.”

Cassia sat on the ground and cried, tears flowed and between sobs she mumbled, “She will never come back.”

Felix moved over towards her and carefully sat next to her. Cassia dropped her head on his shoulder and sobbed. Felix sat still. They sat this way until darkness overcame them. Finally, she looked up at his face. “We should go back,” Felix said to her kindly.

"Ut ego te basia? she whispered to him, moving her face nearer to his. Felix looked at her in surprise, her eyes were closed, and her lips close to his. He touched her hair and kissed her forehead lightly. She smiled and brushed away her tears.

"Grascias tibi. I'll see you tomorrow," he replied softly. She gave a weak smile. Felix picked up his gear and took his horse by the reins. As they left, they walked a little closer together.

***

Not far from the Roman camp, Gaulic tribesman with leaders, Taorio, Vusegus, Alepa, with aspirations to join the war in Italy, stood on a hill watching the Roman caravan. Taorio looked down at the camp. "There are many guards."

Vusegus also had his doubts, but wanted to attack. "Taorio, we have to slow them down. If they arrive at the same time we attack Rome, well, we may be outnumbered."

Alepa the younger looked at Taorio. "Vusegus is right. We have surprise on our side, we attack now."

"Alright Alepa," Taorio responded, "but remind the men that we are not here for women, but for blood. Remember those who have died under the heal of these people. Just kill as many as you can." The three of them left the hilltop woods and went back to their waiting men hidden on the far side of the hill, fully ready for a raid.

Taorio addressed the men, "No captives or booty, men. We can get that in Rome and more. We have to slow these Romans down, kill as many as you can, understand?" There was some general muttering and agreement from the men. Taorio moved to the front of the men. "Remember Argentoratum!" The men raise their swords, axes and bows and called out as one, "Argentoratum!"

The Gauls rode out of the woods and down into the camp as one wave of charging horses. The Roman guards, alerted by the sounds of the horses and fire brands held by riders sounded the trumpet alarm and launched their pilums against the oncoming horsemen. The Gallic horsemen jumped the barriers or clashed with the guards. Those that got into the camp did not stop, but rode right through the camp, cutting down anyone they saw. Decimus, upon hearing the commotion, jumped out of his wagon, calling back to Porcia as he grabbed his sword, "Stay in the wagon! Felix follow me!" Felix grabbed his helmet, sword and shield, jumped out and ran after his father.

Horsemen charged through the camp cutting down Romans, they were being pulled off horses and killed, as others sent burning torches into the wagons. Decimus fought one Gaul after another, cutting down one then the other. Clubbing the riders with his shield while stabbing another with his sword in the other hand. Felix, separated from his father, as the battle raged on, continued to stab riders with his pugio dagger.

Cassia followed her father as he stepped out and fought alongside him, daughter and father killing and stabbing, fighting for their lives. Her pilum spear gone, Cassia picked up a fallen sword and stabbed the nearest horse as it's rider went by. The horse stumbled, the rider fell over the horse's head, and as he landed, she stabbed him then moved on.

Felix ran towards the nearest Roman who had fallen and slashed at the Gaul's back, as he, in turn tried to stab the Roman. Not stopping, Felix grabbed out for a horse's reins, jumped on, and followed other older Romans as they ran over the fallen Gauls where they lay. The Gaelic leader, Taorio, rode by a tent as Alva stepped out. Disregarding his own orders, he clubbed her, picked her up, slung her over his horse and rode out of the camp into the woods.

The remaining Gauls rode through the camp and out the other end stabbing and killing as they went. As Decimus fought, the Gaelic rider came riding up behind him and clubbed him to the ground with one smash to Decimus's unprotected head. He fell where he stood. It was all over. The riders again quickly disappeared into the forests.

Cassia returned to her tent. A dozen guards surrounded the tent. She brushed past them and into the tent to find her father sitting with Centurion Marcus, drinking wine, their uniforms still wet with others' blood. Her father bid her to come to him, he looked her over carefully. "Cassia, who taught you to fight with a sword?"

Cassia, still a mess of sweat, mud, and blood, looked down at her feet. "A friend," she murmured.

"Some friends you have. Here, sit down and have some wine." She sat down and took the offered cup of wine. Her father smiled. "You have your mother's fighting spirit." Marcus said nothing and drank more wine.

Cassia quietly sipped the offered wine, the first time her father had offered her such. "Yes, I suppose so," she said.

Her father turned to Cassia, "Go and get cleaned up, I need to talk to Marcus." She got up and left the tent. Still holding the cup of wine.

Alban sat with Marcus. Both were tired and bloody. More wine was taken, and some offered to Jupiter. Alban touched Marcus's shoulder. "I'm sorry. Now we have lost both our wives."

Marcus wiped the tears from his face. "What is happening? First, we abandon the wall, now this. What more?" He wept again, head in his hands, tears mingling with Gauls' blood on his tunic.

Alban poured more wine. "With most of the troops gone south," said Alban, we need to move faster to the south. I will send out a search party for Alva, but the search party will have to return to us before we decamp, understand?"

"I understand," said Marcus. Slowly both men got up. This journey was not turning out as expected.

After the raid, Felix returned to his wagon. His mother cowered inside but got up when he entered. "Where is your father?" Porcia asked.

"I can't find him," Felix replied.

Porcia looked at his bloody sword. "You fought well my son."

"I was too afraid to stop," he replied, still shaking from the fear of the fight.

"Now you are a warrior my son. Sit and let me feed you," she replied.

"I must clean my sword first." he responded.

"Of course," she replied and started to prepare something for him.

Felix sat down outside, exhausted, and started to clean his sword and knife. A few minutes later six soldiers approached Felix, carrying a body. The first soldier, Sabini, said, "Son of Decimus?"

Felix looked up in surprise from cleaning his sword. "Yes?"

The Romans moved forward and placed the body of Decimus on the ground in front of Felix. Felix looked down at his father, too shocked to even speak. A heavy wound showed on his father's head, where the blood had congealed. "He died a soldier's death," Sabini said. Felix looked at the body.

A second soldier moved forward and handed over Decimus's weapons to Felix. "Here is his scutom and gladius. Use them well. He has joined our comrades in Elysian Fields."

Porcia, upon hearing the voices, stepped out of the wagon, saw the body and screamed. She dropped to the ground and hugged her husband's head and cried out. The first soldier touched Porcia's shoulder. "Mother. Clean the body and anoint him. Place him on the ground naked. We will come for him. Bring wine and one dead chicken for sacrifice. We will carry him to the cremation. From now, your care will become our care." Porcia thanked him between sobs. Sabini looked at Felix. "You are a soldier now, son. You come with us and bring your father's axe. We have many dead and must prepare the funeral pyre with much wood." Porcia stood up and handed Felix an ax. He numbly got up and left with the soldiers.

***

The moon was high in the clear, starlit sky. Huge fires burned with dozens of dead Roman atop of the funeral pyres. The flames lit up the night sky with smoke. Ashes and sparks floated up to the stars with the ghosts of those that had perished. As fires burned, a priest chanted to Jupiter and Juno. "Lo! Jupiter, Juno. Take your sons into your arms! They wait for you in Elysian Fields…" he chanted on.

Commander Alban and other centurions stood quietly in front of the pyres, in respect to the dead. Cassia, standing near her father, saw Felix off to her right, with his mother. Both wearing blackened faces. She walked over to them. Porcia stood closer to the huge fire, wailing for her dead husband, as Felix stood back a bit from the heat of the fire. Cassia come up next to Felix, "Your…father, also?"

Felix looked numbly at her, head down, mumbled, "Yes."

"I'm sorry," she said. "May Mercury guide him."

He said nothing. She took his cold hand into her warm hands. Together, they watched long into the night as the fires burned and the ashes of the dead flew up into the night sky.

***

The wagons and soldiers march on towards the south of Gaul. Someone had lightened the mood by claiming the prize for smelling the sea in the air. The sour mood had lifted, and the pace sped up. Porcia sat on the driver's seat, driving the wagon with Cassia beside her chatting away. "This travelling is so tiring. They say we'll be entering Massilia on the coast in a few days and all will be well then," Cassia went on.

"It's not over yet," replied Porcia. "We have yet to travel the mountains and hills before we get to Rome and only Jupiter knows what we will find there."

"Father says that the Vandals are attacking Rome. I don't think we can enter the city," Cassia replied.

"Well, if that be so, we can go south to my home," Porcia said, smiling. "It will be evening soon. Here, take this dried meat and serve it to your father. Don't forget to add some vinegar and cinnamon to his wine." She handed Cassia some cut meat.

Cassia took the meat. "Thank you. By the way, I'm teaching Felix some Latin."

Porcia looked directly at Cassia. "Don't give him big ideas Cassia."

Cassia jumped off the moving wagon and shouted out, "He has his own will, but I understand what you mean." Cassia walked away towards her father's wagon. Porcia shook her head and muttered to herself.

The camp was once more being made by the soldiers and the wagons were pulled off the roadway. Cassia sat with Felix in the forest. "Your mother knows about us," she said not looking at him directly.

"What is there to know? We are just helping each other," he replied.

"Is that what we are doing?" she said smiling.

Felix stood up. "Are we not?" he replied. "Practice time!" he shouted and handed her a dagger. "This is called a pugio. Guard yourself!" He thrust at her with his pugio. They continued to fight each other until she tripped him up and stuck the pugio into the dirt near his head. Felix, looked up at her. "You are learning fast!" She smiled and helped him up. They brushed themselves off and walked deeper into the woods.

Not far from them, sitting deep in the long grass, sat half a dozen soldiers, taking in the fighting two and placing bets. One soldier handed over some coins to another. "Well, you did say in one month, but I still think that women fighting is strange. Her father would think so too."

The second soldier counted the coins, laughing. "That may be, but she can put up a good fight. He will have his hands full!" They both laughed as they retreated to the camp.

Not far from the camp, near a small river. Cassia and Felix sat together. "You must learn some new phrases today," she said. "Here is the first one. Non gratias tibi aget!"

"No thanks!" he replied.

"But you must!" she scolded. Here, try this one. Where are the toilets? Ubi est sentinis?"

"What do I need that for? We can piss anywhere!" he said.

“Felix!” she replied. “Rome is not Britannia, where anyone can go anywhere. We have buildings you can use. It costs one denarius each time.”

“Ubi est sentinis,” he reluctantly replied. “What else?”

“Where is the Senate? Ubi hoc senatus consulto?” she said.

“What! The senate? Why?” he asked.

“Think high, Felix,” she urged. “Someday you may be a senator!”

“I cannot dream so high,” he replied. “What is another one?”

Cassia got up and washed her feet and face in the river and came back to him. “Here’s another phrase. What is that called. Quid est emim quod cocavit?”

Felix struggled with the sentence. “Quid et emin cod cavait?”

“No! Quid *est* emin *quod cocavit*,” she corrected.

Felix looked up at the sky. “It’s getting late! Did you write these down for me?”

Cassia got up, brushed the burrs from her dress. “Yes, here.” She handed him board with the words inscribed on it. Felix took the board and looked at her carefully, but said nothing.

She took his hand. “Don’t be upset. It will come naturally to you when you start to use it,” she said, looking down at his pants.

“I’ll try,” he replied. They left for the wagons hand in hand.

***

The subcommanders and Marcus stood near the Commander as he once again looked at a map of Gaul and Italy with the help of a lamp.

"We have not done very well on this trip so far. We have yet to reach Rome and already attacks have been made. We don't need any more of that! Soon we will be into Massilia." He pointed to the map and Lugdunum. "Lugdunum has been sacked recently by the Germanics. We will not stop there, but press on. Regardless of wagons and families, we will force march, day and night until we get there, it's not so far. I do not want to see any more losses. Tell your families and men to be ready. We start out tonight and stop only when we reach the city. Understood?"

"What about wagons that break down?" Marcus asked. "Leave the wagons and whoever is with them. Keep going. Dismissed," Alban ordered. The men saluted and left tent in haste.

The camp was woken up. Horses made ready for the soldiers and wagons. Men donned their armor and weapons and shouldered their gear. Fires were put out. Finally, the trumpet sounded, and the forced, quick march started in earnest. The wagons moved as fast as they could go. The soldiers marched behind and in front of the wagons. Behind them came riders and in front, forward scouts. The night wore on, dark rain clouds moved in.

Porcia pushed her horse to move ever faster, not seeing the hole in the road for the dust, drove the front right wheel into the hole. The wheel snapped sideways, broke off, causing the wagon to stop and fall over sideways. Both Porcia and Cassia fell out onto the now wet road. Soldiers looked on as they passed, but no one stopped to help. Felix riding ahead, heard the commotion and rode back to see what had happened. He stopped and jumped off his horse to help them.

Felix looked down at the fallen women as he extended his hand to help them up. "Are you alright?!"

Both women get up off the ground. "Oh Felix!" Cassia lamented. "The wheel has broken. They will leave us behind!"

Porcia looked at the broken wheel. "Felix, can we fix this?" she asked.

"I can try but we need to get a fire going. It's too dark to fix without some light. But what about your father?" he replied.

"He thinks I am asleep in the forward wagon. We must hurry!"

Porcia pointed to Cassia. "Stop talking and help me," she ordered. The women both pulled out the new wheel and rolled it towards Felix. More and more soldiers passed them, shouting out encouragement and good fortune until there were none left to pass the wagon.

Felix tried to find the tools inside the wagon but lacked the light to see what he needed. The clouds had blotted out the fading light and rain was making it even harder. The inside of the wagon was a mess with everything upside down. He came out of the wagon. "We must wait till dawn or move now. Already the soldiers cannot be seen."

"We cannot wait here!" Cassia cried. "My father will be so angry if he finds me gone!"

Felix looked at his mother. Porcia looked at them both. "Alright, then we use my wagon horses and leave now." Felix got their horses ready as the women pulled their capes out of the wagon, along with some food and water. Porcia handed Felix his father's cape, along with his tunic, sword, and short dagger. Then the rain came in haste.

They moved forward, following the trail of the other wagons and soldiers, mile after mile. The horses tiring, moved ever slower. Finally in the rain and dark, they reached a fork in the road. Felix slid off his horse and looked for tracks of the wagons and men. The rain fell even harder, which made seeing the trail impossible but for the road stones. "I can't decide which way they went," he shouted back.

Cassia shouted out, "We must choose!"

Porcia called to him, "Go right?"

"Wait!" Felix shouted. Looking at the bushes, he found a small banner from one of the kind soldiers, tied to the bushes, marking the right way. "You are right, Mother, they went right!" He jumped on his tired horse, but the animal refused to budge. Felix jumped off, grabbed the reins, and pulled the horse while he ran beside it and the women riding their horses into the night.

Dawn came and the rain stopped. The women were half asleep on their horses, which by now were trotting slowly with Felix in front. Felix saw an old wall nearby the forest and stopped. Exhausted from walking in the rain, he moved towards the trees, found a comfortable place behind the old wall, well hidden from the road. The women dismounted. Porcia grabbed his sword and chopped some fur branches down to make two beds. Felix, flopped down next to a tree, while Cassia hobbled the horses.

Cassia came back to find Porcia making the makeshift beds. “Why two beds?” she asked.

“You and Felix over their together. He needs rest and warmth. He may yet have to fight, you understand?” she replied

“Yes but—” Cassia sputtered.

“No buts, help me pick him up,” Porcia demanded. They both grabbed him and placed him on the branch bed. Porcia left Cassia and fell onto her bed and was soon snoring. Cassia looked at her and then at Felix who was fast asleep. His wet clothes stuck to his body and hers also. She took the horse blankets off the horses, took most of his clothes off and hers, then pulled the blankets over them and was soon asleep.

***

The sun came up. The rain had stopped and the trees shed their wetness into the shimmering air. Cassia’s almost naked body was very close to Felix. Her arm slung over his body. Felix woke up, blinked, and turned over. His face showed surprise as he saw that it was not his mother’s, but Cassia’s, arm resting on him. He felt every inch of her warmth. His body was now fully awake, lips inches apart from hers, he gently kissed her.

She responded without opening her eyes, “You seemed to have recovered your energy,” she said. Felix smiled. Her eyes opened slowly and she stared at him. “Don’t get ideas,” she whispered as she started to get up.

Nearby, Porcia jumped up. “Hey you two! We must go!” She saw their clothes hanging on branches and took them off and threw them towards where they lay, turned her back and walked away. Cassia hid under the horse blanket, while Felix jumped up, got dressed, then took the horses to the roadway where his mother waited, staring at her son. Cassia came over but avoided looking at them both. “Let’s go,” Porcia said, and with that, they all got on their horses and headed down the road, further and further until they reached Massilia.

MASSILIA

The commander along with the Duce of Gaul and Centurion Marcus, sat in the luxurious south villa admiring the Mediterranean Sea while sipping wine. It was a long way from where they had just come. None of them were smiling. The duce grabbed some more grapes with his fat hands. “There have been to many changes in my lifetime,” he said, “maybe too many. Look, yesterday Alexandria was the shining example and now it’s underwater. Constantinople is now our shiny new capital, and the Christians…oh for Jupiter’s sake!” He said in disgust, “well, and now Britannia!”

Marcus, enjoying a massage from a slave girl remarked, “Magnus Maximus started that off! If he hadn’t pulled troops out of Britannia, we would still be there today. And what about the Christians? That meeting in Constantinople has done what? We should have taken care of that lot a long time ago.”

A servant came into the room and whispered into the commander’s ear. “Send them in,” he ordered.

Standing in front of them looking rather sheepish, stood three, dirty, wet, and tired people. The commander looked over his daughter. “Cassia. Your mother is gone and here I am worrying that the same fate had taken you! Just what were you doing?”

Cassia looked at her feet. “I was helping—” she started.

Her father interrupted her, his eyes fixed on Felix. "Is this the rabbit supplier and the one that helped you both?"

"Yes," she replied, looking at Felix.

"What's your name boy?" the commander demanded.

"Felix, sir," Felix answered.

Looking at Porcia, the commander asked, "And you?"

"I am Porcia, wife of Decimus," Porcia replied.

"He was a good man," the commander said, as he waved off the masseuse and sat down. "May the Goddess Matronae protect you. My wagon is now yours to use. You will now serve Cassia. Get cleaned up and try to stay out of trouble. Felix, you stay a minute."

The two left the room. The commander looked Felix up and down. "Thank you son, for taking care of my daughter. You are now on my payroll as my wagon guard. The protection of my daughter is your duty. Do you understand?"

"Yes, sir. Thank you. sir," Felix replied quickly.

"You will report directly to Centurion Marcus, here," the commander went on. "He will set your pay and see to your training. Dismissed soldier."

"Yes, sir. Gratias tibi, sir!" Felix replied as he backed out of the room, bowing and saluting in confusion.

The duce looked at the men. "Rome is suffering, Commander. I need to ask you to move your troops along as soon as you can, please."

The commander put down his glass. "The men need time to clean up and rest and we need to resupply, but I think it best I take most of our troops, and the Spanish troops who will arrive today, with me and let the families follow behind. They slow us down."

Marcus sat up. "Leave the caravan unprotected?"

"I'll leave some of the Spanish troops to protect them," Commander Alban replied. "We are in safe territory now. If they make haste, they will only be a few days behind us and can avoid Rome and move further south."

"You can leave the families here if you like," the duce offered.

"That would be preferable," the commander said. "I can leave a cohort of eight hundred men to protect them."

Marcus looked up in trepidation. "These troops from Spain are Germanics right?"

"Yes," replied Commander Alban.

"Well, we can't leave Roman troops here, while their families are being attacked in Italy. These Germanics have been loyal for a long time now, we have to trust them. Duce, what are your thoughts?"

The duce got up, poured them all some more wine. "Leave the Germanics here, we will be alright. You had better move quickly. I'll see to your supplies." A servant walked into the room with more wine, and plates of food. The duce stood up. "A toast to Rome!" They all stood and raised their glasses. "To Rome!"

***

Porcia, Cassia, and Felix loaded up Cassia's wagon for the move eastward. Felix told Cassia what orders he had received. "What!" she said, "you are my guard! My father said that!?"

"Yes," Felix said, smiling. "And with pay under Centurion Marcus."

Porcia stopped to look at them both. "Teutates, Esus, Taranis! The Gods protect you both!"

"And who are these Gods?" asked Cassia.

"Local Gods for local problems. Now, let's get this wagon loaded up shall we?" Porcia ordered. Felix and Cassia got back to work, loading the wagon up.

As they were loading up, a man stood on a box and called out to all the wagon families. Asking them to convene near him. Acting like a news crier, he called out to the gathering crowd, "Come to me, come to me! There is new news! Come over and listen!" The people stopped loading and came over to him. He continued, "The duce has ordered all to stay here. The troops from Spain will protect us. The other troops will leave tomorrow, for Rome needs their help quickly. Happy news! Rejoice and unpack!" He got off the box and left. The crowd murmured, some worrying and some happy about the plan.

"What?" Cassia said in surprise. "We are to stay here! What will we do?"

"Your father is needed in Rome. The duce will provide for you. Maybe he will give you a nice room to use," Porcia replied.

“Yes!” said Felix. “And I will stand guard outside the door!”

“I don’t need a guard,” Cassia snapped.

“Maybe, maybe not. But I must follow your father’s orders,” Felix snapped back.

“The fox in charge of the chicken house,” smiled Porcia. “Come on both of you, we have much to do,” she said, as she made moved towards the duce’s villa.

***

A few days later, the troops assembled on the road leading to Rome, and lined up ready to go. Commander Alban gave the orders to march. The trumpets sounded the call and the quick march sounded out, as the commander passed the crowd on horseback. Seeing his daughter, he called her over to him as he slowed down and leaned over to talk to her. “I’ll be back soon enough. Worry not and take care of yourself, alright?” With that he continued onward, leaving Cassia crying at the side of the road.

Felix and Porcia offered comfort to Cassia. “Dry your tears my dear,” Porcia said. “Rome will not fall and your father will be back soon.” Cassia’s face did not show the same conviction.

***

A few days later, Porcia, Felix, and Cassia finished putting Cassia’s things into her new room in the villa. The villa overlooked the Mediterranean Sea and a beach could be seen below the cliff. Cassia opened a window and looked out. "What a beautiful day and what gorgeous smelling flowers! I think I will swim!"

Felix stood guard by her open door. "You can't swim here! The waters are cold and dangerous!"

Cassia laughed and joked, "My loyal guard! This is a warm sea, not an England sea. One can play in the waters here. You must close the door and guard me as my father ordered!" She pointed to the door. Felix, looking vexed by her orders, closed the door.

Porcia walked about admiring the décor in Casia's room. "It's a beautiful villa. We are so blessed. I saw a water spring nearby, the Goddess Coventina lives nearby. We are protected."

"I hope so," Cassia replied "I am tired of the road and its dangers. Did you see those Germanic guards outside? They looked so…unfriendly."

Porcia laid out Cassia's dresses. "Their salt comes from Rome, don't worry, they will protect us also."

Cassia pranced about. "In that case, I will walk to the beach!"

"Shall I join you?" asked Porcia.

"No. I will take my guard."

"My son will protect you with his life," his mother said.

"So be it! What shall I wear!?" Cassia shouted back, feeling like a commander's daughter again.

Cassia and Felix walked down to the beach. She, with some food in a basket, and he, with his weapons and shield. As they reached the beach, Felix looked at the water. "Now you will swim?" he asked with a worried look.

She laughed. "You must protect me, even in the water! Turn your back!" she ordered.

Felix stared at her, then turned his back. Looking the other way, he shouted back, "It must be dangerous!"

She laid a blanket on the beach and did not reply, but quickly removed all her clothes, then jumped into the sea, naked.

Felix, hearing her jump in, turned around to see her splashing about in the water. Cassia called out, laughing, "You must come in also! You cannot protect me over there!"

Felix looked at his weapons and shield, then at her playing in the water. He looked about for danger then seeing none, put his weapons near the blanket and stripped down. Felix called to her, "Is it warm?"

Cassia laughed. "Very warm! Hurry up!" She averted her eyes, somewhat, as he disrobed and jumped in. She swam over to him as he struggled in the water. "Don't drown, my guard!" she laughed as she spat water in his direction. He spat out sea water. She swam around him laughing at his efforts to swim.

"It's so warm!" he commented.

They swam under the water and splashed about for a while. Finally, Cassia came to him in the shallow water, grabbed his neck, and pushed him under the water playfully. Underwater the only thing he could see was her naked body, causing him to immediately come up, sputtering and coughing water out. He grabbed her shoulders and pulled her towards him and kissed her. She clung to him and returned his kisses. Together, they came out of the water, lay down on the blanket and softly, but wildly, they kissed each other as they both explored each other's body, finally bonding on the hot sand. Sometime later, they both lay exhausted and holding each other till the sun became too hot. Running back into the water, they washed each other than departed for the villa, tired and happy for a change.

***

The next afternoon, Cassia and Porcia prepared to make a new summer dress and calcei boots for riding with Felix. Felix knocked on the door of her room. Porcia walked over to the door and opened it. "She will be ready soon, wait my son. Women take time to look their best."

"Look…" he started. "We're going to the—" Porcia cut him off giving him "the look." Seeing her face, he turned around. "I'll be waiting," he complained and walked outside to the horses.

Cassia came out of the building with Porcia behind her. Felix took one look at her and lost his sour look. It was the first time he had seen her look like a country lady. He took hold of her horse as she got into it. Astride, she looked down at his mother. "We'll be back before supper."

With a concerned look, Porcia handed a small satchel of food to Cassia. "Be careful." she said, as they departed for the countryside.

The couple rode off out of the villa and a while later near some grape fields, they stopped the horses inside the fields, tied them to a grapevine, and hand in hand walked to a small clearing. In the midst of the grape field, they threw down a blanket and opened the bag of food and wine bota bag. Felix casually picked a grape from a vine nearby, "So this is where wine comes from," he said, admiring the grape.

Cassia took the grape and popped it into Felix's open mouth. "There are many kinds of wines and grapes. My father says that the best wine comes from here." They both lay on the blanket, cast off their cares and finished off the wine as Cassia popped grapes into his mouth.

After they had finished eating, they lay together looking up at the sky. "What will happen to Rome?" Felix asked, gazing up at the clouds.

"Rome is Rome," Cassia replied. "All will be fine, it has been the center of the world for a thousand years. Even before the Egyptian Queen, Cleopatra, my teacher told me."

"Yes, but why are all the troops leaving Gaul and Britannia after so many years? Is it not strange?" he went on.

"Only you are strange!" she replied laughing. "Don't worry, my father will take care of those Vandals!"

"And I will take care of you," he said in a serious voice.

"Really? Kind sir," she said, "and how will you do that? Are you rich?"

"No," he said.

"You have a title?" she asked teasingly.

"No," he said, sitting up.

"What do you have then?" she asked.

“Well, I have my mother,” he replied.

“And…”she prompted.

“And…you,” he said shyly.

Cassia rolled over to face him, took his face into her hands, and kissed him tenderly. “Yes, kind sir, you do,” she replied releasing his lips. They embraced as the sun started to set lower in the sky.

Sometime later, they woke up to the sound of their horses’ nervousness. Felix got up and looked about, then looked again to the south. “That’s funny,” he said, looking south.

Cassia, half dreamily asked, “What is?”

“That!” he said pointing. They both looked to the south. Smoke rose from the area of the city. “I don’t remember seeing black smoke before. It’s too much smoke. We had better return carefully. I fear something is wrong. Let’s take the path through the fields, not the road.”

They packed up, mounted their horses and left via a trail through the fields. As they approached the city, more smoke could be seen, and cries of help heard. Carefully, they got off their horses and walked with the horses through the fields. Stopping behind some bushes they could see that the city was in mayhem. The Germanic troops were everywhere. Burning the houses, dragging young women out and raping them. Carrying goods out of the houses and killing anyone they could find.

Cassia turned to Felix. “What about your mother! We need to get to your villa!” They got onto their horses and rode through the streets at full gallop, around the soldiers before they could be stopped. Arriving at the villa. They both entered the house. The house had been ransacked and the duce lay dead on the floor. They called out as they entered and went from room to room. "Mother! Mother!" Felix cried out.

"Porcia where are you!?" Cassia shouted. A cry came from under Cassia's bed. Felix looked carefully under the bed. Porcia lay there quivering.

"Mother, come out please!" he implored.

His mother came out from under the bed, still shaking. "Oh, Felix, they've killed the duce! Took everything! I had to hide…"

"They are destroying the town. We have to leave here now!" Felix told her.

"But to where!?" she asked.

"To Rome," he replied as he turned to Cassia. "Quickly! Cassia get a bag and fill it with food. Mother you help her. I'll look for another horse."

Felix went out to the courtyard. Night was setting in and all about he could see house fires, looting, and killing. Felix found a third horse running about with no rider, caught it and brought it to the courtyard. The women were waiting. Cassia had dressed again in men's riding clothes, and had a short sword, bow, and a quiver of arrows that she found inside for herself and Felix. They got onto the horses and fled into the night, down to the beach and followed the beach eastward as far as they could go.

***

The next day, the weather was still good, the ocean calm with waves beating on the shores. The three slept well into the morning, exhausted from the day before. Finally, Felix woke up the others. "We had better leave this place," he said. They all got up, ate quickly and then without a word, mounted their horses and prepared to leave the area.

"Maybe we can ride all the way Rome," Cassia said.

"Maybe," Porcia said, shifting in her saddle. "But if there are problems there, we should go south of Rome to your great grandfather's home in Matera. There is nothing there for the Vandals, we'll be safe."

"There is no need for that," Cassia replied, "my father will take care of everything. Just wait, as soon as we near Rome, we will be safe."

"Maybe," said Felix, "but these Germanics, who knows which way they will turn. How far is it to Rome?"

"About four days by horse," his mother replied. "If we encounter no delays, we will reach the mountains in two days."

"Then let's start," Cassia replied nervously.

With that, they rode out of the beach and headed towards Italy. After riding hard all day, they made camp near a river coming from a nearby mountain range. Porcia busied herself making a small fire to make something to eat. Felix tethered horses and groomed them. Cassia sat near Porcia, cutting up a rabbit. She called out to Felix, "We need some wild onions, can you find some?"

Porcia called to her, "I'll go. Felix does not know an onion from a mushroom! I'll get some." She walked off into the nearby bushes. Felix made a face and continued cleaning his horse blanket from burrs. "Do you know what lies in those mountains?" he asked Cassia.

"A wide road that leads to Rome, as all do," she replied.

"I think we should take another way over the mountains," he replied.

"With the horses, can we take another way?" she asked.

"We can ask my mother. She may know," Felix answered.

"Do you remember your Latin?" Cassia asked as she stoked the small fire.

"I'm not worried about that right now. It's those dark mountains. I don't like mountains."

Porcia came back with wild onions and other plants. She put them down and started to clean them for the rabbit stew. "Mother, do you know another way through these mountains by horseback?"

"Yes," said Porcia. "We had to use a path when we came to Gaul, due to heavy rains. I will lead the way."

"I'm afraid of what's in the mountains," Felix said in front of Cassia.

Cassia got up. "I'm going relieve myself." She pulled up some long grass and walked into the bushes a distance away. As soon as she was gone, Felix's mother slapped Felix in the face. Shocked then angered he got up. Porcia also stood up and faced him. "You must never show fear in front of Cassia. You understand?"

"Alright but there is no need—" he protested.

Porcia interrupted him. “There is need! There is no fear like fear of the unknown. You are now the man of this family and she may be your wife and bear your children, the way you two have been going on. Show her you will protect her!”

“Well, maybe—” he replied.

“No maybe! You carry your father’s name and sword. Don’t forget that!” Cassia returned. Porcia looked at Cassia. “Cassia. Felix says we need to guard. I will take first turn after supper.” Porcia smiled at Felix.

“Oh, alright. I’ll take next then,” Felix half-heartedly smiled back.

They all bedded down without further word. His mother stood near the horses and watched over the sleeping couple.

***

The next morning, before the sun was fully up, they cleaned up, finished off the rabbit stew, poured water over the fire, got on their horses and left the camp. Without a word, they rode into the mountains. They rode all day with Porcia in the lead, Cassia next, then Felix, into the dark forest foothills then slowly ascended into the mountains. By the time they entered Italy, the sea could be seen as they rode along steep cliffs dropping to the sea on the narrowest of paths for the horses to tread. One wrong move by the horses and that would be the end of them.

Finally, as late afternoon set, they stopped near a creek in some quiet woods. Porcia got off her horse and immediately went into the bushes to relieve herself.

Felix took the three horses to the stream to let them drink. "It's not so bad is it? There are few using this trail," he said to Cassia.

Cassia rubbed her sore bum and legs. "I would be happy if we met no one until we got to Rome."

Suddenly the bushes parted. Porcia was back flanked by two men. Felix turned towards her and stopped. Cassia, washing her face in the stream, looked up, saw his face, turned and saw what he was staring at. Standing next to Porcia holding her arms, were two men, one tall and one average. Their age seemed to be very old, their eyes seemed weary. Their long robes and beards seemed out of place somehow with their short swords and a small wooden crucifixes around their necks. They released Porcia. She quickly moved close to Felix.

The tall man asked Cassia, "Quod nomens tibi est? What's your name?"

Cassia replied, "Tibi est Cassia, Felix, Porcia."

"Di dove sie? Where are you from?" he asked.

"Dall Inghilterra. From England," Cassia replied.

The two men exchanged glances. Cassia looked at them both. "Parli Latino? Do you speak Latin?"

The short man spat on the ground. "No. Italiano."

The tall one pointed. "Sedersi. Mangiare. Sit down. Eat."

He handed the three of them some beef jerky from his belt pouch. They carefully took it, not taking their eyes off the two men.

Felix, rested one hand on his sword as Cassia pointed to the ground. "Lei grazie. Thank you." They all sat down, carefully.

The short man, pointed with beef jerky at the end of his knife. "Dove stai andando? Where are you going?"

Porcia cut in, "Roma. Rome."

The tall one said, "Roma e morta, Vandals e Mephitis. Rome is dead from the Vandals and malaria."

Cassia's mouth dropped, "E morta!? Dead?!"

"Qual e il tou Dio?" the short one asked.

"What did he ask?" Felix asked.

"Rome is dead from malaria and he offers us some more beef jerky," Cassia replied.

Felix, Cassia and Porcia looked at each other very carefully. "Teutates, Esus,Taranis," Porcia said.

The tall one laughed, "Sciocchi! Siamo Cristiani. C'e un solo Dio!"

Felix looked at Cassia. "What did he say?"

"He said, 'you need to study Latin more!' " she replied.

"Really?!" Felix asked.

"No," Cassia said. "He said 'they are Christians and there is only one God.' "

"Well," said Felix most sincerely, "he must be a very lonely God then."

The short one pointed to Felix. "Sie sua moglie? Are you his wife?"

"Non ancora. Not yet," Cassia replied.

"Sciocchi, siamo cristiani! Fools, we are Christian!" the short one said again.

Cassia looked at the man but did not comment. The men got up. Felix again put his hand on his sword started to pull it out.

The tall man backed away. "Partiamo ora. Voi viaggia verso la morte. Torna da dove sei venuto da. Let's go now. You travel to death. Go back to where you came from."

Then without further comment or goodbyes, the two men walked into the forest and disappeared. Porcia looked at Felix. "We should leave this place."

"Yes," he replied.

"What strange people," Cassia remarked.

"Yes, let's leave," Felix replied.

They got back onto their horses. "We may arrive in Italy soon!" Porcia called out to them and with that, they rode off down the path in the woods towards the southeast and into Italy. As the light was fading, they came down from the mountains and onto a side road, closer to the sea. They made camp, hidden somewhat in the woods, and a small fire was made. Then they sat there, too tired to talk. There was little food left except jerky.

Finally Cassia spoke. “My stomach feels funny,” she said, as she examined her belly.

“Ha!” laughed Felix. “I’m losing weight. You must be eating all the food!”

Porcia got up and felt Cassia’s stomach. “I’ll make some hot herb water for us to drink,” she offered.

Felix also got up and gathered his hunting bows. “Mother, we will be back soon. We’ll see what we can hunt,” Then, looking at Cassia, “Take up your bow and arrows. We go hunting, before it is too dark to find something.” She got up and got her bow and followed him into the woods. They headed downhill and found a small creek. There they squatted and waited. Then, through the fading light a small deer came into view.

Felix touched Cassia’s shoulder and woke her out of her stupor. She looked up and looked ahead. Whispering, Felix pointed to the deer, “Careful now. Take an arrow and aim for the top of the front leg.”

Cassia saw the deer, took up her bow, drew an arrow carefully from her quiver, put it into her bow, lined up the shot and released the arrow. Her aim was true, the arrow went right into the heart of the deer. “I got it!” she cried with joy.

“Mm, not bad, now the hard part,” Felix replied as they approached the deer. She gave a wry grin. They cut up the deer quickly, then with both carrying it, they took it back to the camp.

Seeing the deer, Porcia jumped up. “Ah! My mighty hunters! Good work both of you!” They dropped the deer parts on the grass in front of her.

Cassia looked down at the deer. “How will we keep this from going bad?” she asked.

“We need to stay here a few days,” Porcia replied. “I’ll show you how to cure the meat to jerky, then we will have enough until we get to Rome. Porcia went over to the deer. “Felix, tie a rope between the trees and get some wet and dry wood together.”

“And I?” asked Cassia.

“Get your knife. We have much to cut up tonight,” Porcia replied as she started to hack the meat into smaller pieces. Felix soon returned with wood. “Son, make a smoke fire under that rope and Cassia, take these cut pieces and put them on the rope.” Soon the meat was cut into long thin slices and swinging on the rope over a smoky fire. The three looked at the meat, drying over the fire. Everyone was tired.

Cassia looked at her hands. “I smell of blood.”

Porcia looked at Felix. “We’ll go to the creek.”

“And I will guard your supper and eat nothing till you come back,” said Felix as he lay down and closed his eyes, not waking up till the dawn cold forced him to. The women having returned, slept nearby.

***

The mountain fog was thick in the forest as Porcia woke up and stoked with the still smoking fire. “Keep the fires going till the sun rises,” she said to Felix as he awoke. “We’ll put it out then, as someone may see it.”

Two mornings later, Porcia cut a hole in the dried deer stomach. Then together they squashed berries into the meat, then pushed the meat into the stomach. Finally, Porcia sucked out all the air and sealed the hole. “That should last us a while,” she said as she washed down the last of the wine.

They ate breakfast, rested, waited for the sun to come up and the fog to disperse before breaking camp. Cassia lay down on her blanket looking at the treetops. “Are we refugees?” she asked no one in particular.

“No, of course not,” Porcia said, laying beside her. “We are seeking shelter from the storms of man. We are going to live the good life in the land of promise, I am sure of that.”

“What will happen in Britannia and Gaul? Will the Gauls or Germanic stake over our forts?” Cassia went on.

Felix sat, watching the woods opposite her. “I will return with a force of Rome and put them all in their place!” he said, forcefully.

“But what if we arrive in Rome and there is a wall blocking our way?” Cassia asked.

“What wall?” Felix asked.

“My father says that Rome has a big wall around it, to keep out the Vandals and refugees,” Cassia replied.

“But,” Porcia stated firmly, “we are not refugees!”

Cassia sat up. "But, do they know that we are from Britannia. Do they know that we are really Romans?"

Felix looked at his mother. "Mother, is Roman but my father was born in Britannia, as was I."

"You both worry about nothing. Anyone can see that we are all Romans, papers or no papers," Porcia scolded them both.

"I'm not so—" Cassia started to say.

Felix stood up suddenly and put his finger to his lips to hush her. Then took out his sword and looked into the woods where the road was. Small eyes could be seen between the trees. Cassia looked at Felix and jumped up and took hold of her sword. Porcia got up and quickly backed up.

Cassia called out, "Who are you? Chi sei?"

There was no movement.

"Chi sei? Uscire di li! Come out!" Cassia repeated.

Figures started to emerge. Five children and two adults, a man and woman. All very badly dressed, and all in need of a bath and food.

The man moved forward. "Iniuriam nullam in animo habemus! We mean no harm!"

Felix approached the man and checked him for weapons. There was only a small knife in his belt, which Felix allowed him to keep.

"Da dove vieni? Where are you coming from?"Cassia asked.

Again the man replied, "Non lontano da Roma. Not far from Rome."

"He is from Rome?" Felix asked.

"Nearby," Cassia replied.

Porcia pointed to the food. "Hai fame? Are You Hungry?"

"Filii esurientes. Hungry children," the man said.

Porcia pointed to the ground. "Sede et comede. Sit and eat."

They all sat down and took the meat and water offered to them. In quick time the offered food was finished. Felix asked Cassia, "What is happening to Rome?"

Cassia translated, "Cosa succede a Roma?"

The old man swallowed and replied, "Romae tribus impugnatur ab Vandal. Movere bellum contra nos evitare malaria. Movere debet contra orientem."

Cassia looked at Felix. "He says that Rome is under attack from Vandals and that there are so many dead from malaria, so we must move eastward to avoid fighting and malaria."

Cassia pointed to the family. "Vai a lavarti. Ce e un ruscello laggiu. Go wash. There's a stream down there.

The family got up and left to wash up. Felix looked at the others. "We need to leave as soon as the sun is up, if there are so many refugees, we will be feeding all who we meet!"

Porcia looked at the hanging meat. "Let us pack up this meat, leave them some and leave as Felix says." They got up and started to pack the meat into saddlebags and prepared to leave. When the family returned to the camp, Felix offered them more food. They took it and all settled down to rest with Porcia taking first watch. The sun was now up, the fog dispersed, and all got up. The children of the refugees were fed then they got ready to go.

The father looked at Porcia. “Gracias tibi, gracias!” he said three times, bowed, then the family departed down the path towards the west. Felix and Cassia loaded up the horses. Porcia put out the fire then they sat on their horses and planned.

“What to do if we meet more refugees?” Felix asked.

“Nothing!” replied his mother. “They must fend for themselves. We care for ourselves.” Felix and Cassia looked at each other, shrugged as Porcia started out, leading the way onto the trail and southward towards Rome.

AUGUST 24TH, AD 410

As they moved south, their speed of movement became slower and slower as they were forced to constantly watch for marauding bands of Goths or worse still, Vandals. They were back on the seacoast, sticking to hidden, less-used trails. The trail became very narrow and old. Blocks of stone on both sides, like walls, covered with moss. This part of the coastline trail was rarely used, but was never far from the more popular routes.

They rode in silence most of the day. Finally, exhausted more from fear of being discovered rather than the ride, they took refuge and rested above a cliff that overlooked a flat area and took an afternoon nap. As they slept, a group of Gaul raiders moved into the flat area by horseback with carts carrying slaves and stolen goods from raids. The noise was enough to wake up Porcia. She sat up, saw the Gaul's and poked Felix awake, pointing towards the cliff's edge. Felix woke up, rubbed his eyes and walked over to the cliff side to see what the noise was. He saw Gauls nearby and immediately fell to the ground and hid. "Jupiter protect us!" he muttered. The Gaul's were too busy to notice him as they stopped and prepared to rest.

Felix crawled away from the cliff side and woke up Cassia. "Wake up and follow me carefully," he whispered to her. The three of them crawled to the cliff side. Below them was a small creek and flat land with a wagon trail nearby. Three of the Gauls were talking to each other, standing on the road near one of the wagons, not far from the creek below the cliff. Taorio looked at the booty in the wagon and commented to his men, "We have done well my friends and soon we will take Rome."

Vusegus laughed. "Getting these slaves and booty home is going to need more wagons!"

Alepa turned to the slave woman. "Slave! Get more water and hurry it up." The woman got up and walked slowly towards the creek with a small wooden bucket. As she reached the creek, Cassia and Felix saw her face clearly. Cassia reacted with a shock. The woman was very skinny and in bad shape, but she could see that it was or looked like Alva.

"It's Centurion Marcus's wife!" Cassia whispered.

Felix quickly covered her mouth with his hand and whispered in her ear, "It may look like her but if it is not, we'll all be killed today." Cassia nodded her head in agreement but looked at the woman as she bent down to get water.

The woman stood up and walked back to the men. She gave the water to Alepa. He drank the water then slapped her backside. "Get more water!"

The three watched from the cliff top as she walked back to the creek with her bucket. Cassia whispered madly, "We must get her out."

Porcia moved closer to the edge. "Then we must do it now. There will not be another chance."

Felix waited until the woman again reached the creek and tossed a small stone at her. She did not hear or see it.

He tossed another.

Alva looked about, but not up. He tossed a third and it landed right on her head. That caused her to look up. Alva looked up at the faces and Cassia looked down at her. Eye to eye contact was made. The woman looked shocked and stared upwards. "Wa…wa…" Alva cried.

Cassia put her finger to her mouth. Alva look up again. Felix pointed to the trail on the right that led to the top of the cliff. Alva understood, dropped the bucket and looked behind her. The Gauls were in deep in conversation and laughter. Alva moved to the trail and went up to meet the three. There they all hugged in near silence, the women weeping.

Felix interrupted them. "We must ride now!" They got on their horses, Alva riding with Cassia, and left in haste. They rode far into the day, leaving the mountains and did not rest until they reached a small, tucked away beach. Here, they dismounted and made camp. Alva was in bad shape and exhausted from her experience as a slave.

Porcia looked down at Alva, laying on a blanket. "She looks exhausted. I will ride alone to a small town not far from here called Rapollo and trade some meat for fish." No one stopped her. She got on her horse and left.

Cassia looked at Alva. "Alba we need to wash you. Can you walk?"

"I think so," Alva replied. Felix and Cassia pulled her to her feet and helped her into the water. Cassia washed her as Felix made a comfortable camp and took care of the horses. Completely washed, Cassia took Alva back to the camp near the beach and lay her on a horse blanket.

Alva looked at Cassia. “My child, how is it that you found me?”

“It was by chance. I suppose we were moving the same way as the Gauls were,” Cassia replied as she dried Alva’s hair.

“I never ever thought we would meet again. I cried every night,” Alva said, as tears started to fall.

“Oh Alva!” Cassia said and started to cry also.

Felix made himself busy making a fire and making supper. The women held each other and cried until there were no more tears to shed.

Later that evening, Porcia came back with some fish and herbs. She soon cooked up the fish, prepared the herbs in hot water and gave it to Cassia. Cassia spoon-fed Alva, bit by bit.

Clearing her mouth, Alva said, “I will slow you all down. Leave me here. I am alright now.”

“Never,” replied Cassia. “You will come with us.”

Alva turned to Porcia. “Thank you for your kindness.”

Porcia smiled back. “Please sleep now. We will leave tomorrow. You are safe with us Alva.” The night came. The fire burned down, they all slept.

The waves beat on the shoreline, then sometime at midnight with a million stars shining above, Alva woke up, kissed Cassia on the forehead and placed a necklace on her blanket. Then slowly, she walked to the water, disrobed, looked up at the stars and swam out into the water and slowly disappeared under the waves.

Cassia woke up at first light, turned over and found the necklace. She immediately looked towards Alva's bed. With a cry she got up and looked about for her. Felix and Porcia woke up and looked about. Cassia found Alva's footprints heading towards the water's edge and her clothes nearby. Porcia held Cassia as they cried. Porcia looked towards Felix. "We must leave. We have to travel by four small towns and can get something to eat."

They washed their tears away, mounted up and left the camp. By noontime they had arrived at the hills overlooking Rome. Smoke could be seen rising high into the sky. They found a wall, tied up the horses and climbed a nearby hill to look at Rome, off in the distance.

Felix looked at the smoke. "That does not look good."

"Somewhere down there is my father," Cassia remarked in a dull voice.

"I can see Roman's camped outside the walls. We should go and see. We need to get closer," Porcia said.

They turned, got on their horses and moved down the hillside closer to Rome. They could see the troops and, in the distance, what seemed to be figures laying in the sun…many figures. Cassia pinched her nose. "The smell is terrible and what is going on over there?"

"I think they are dead men and horses," Felix remarked. "Many of them."

"They are dead men, but who's dead? And the gates appear to be closed. Why close the gates to the city?" she worried.

Cassia pointed. "See over there! Those are from the north! Those flags."

"Vandals?!" Felix asked. They all remained silent. Felix spied a few Roman soldiers walking on the road. "I will ask those soldiers what is going on."

"We'll come with you." They rode over to the soldiers.

"Excuse me!" Felix called out from his horse. "What is happening in the city?"

The soldier looked at him like he was stupid. "Where have you been hiding. The city is closed. Malaria is everywhere with many dead. No one goes in or out. The Vandals have control of most roads and are cutting off the food supply."

"Have you heard anything about the soldiers from the frontier?" Cassia asked.

"What frontier?" the soldier put to her.

"Hadrian's Wall, Britannia." Felix said proudly.

"Under Commander Alban?" the soldier asked.

"Yes!" shouted Cassia

"We offered his body to Jupiter yesterday. And most of his men. They were decimated by the Gauls and Vandals, and others died from malaria. Tarry not in this area," the soldier advised. Cassia cried out. All three of them lowered their head. “I must go,” the soldier said. “May Jupiter protect you all!” he called out as he moved on down the road.

Cassia would have fallen from her horse in shock if Felix had not caught her and lowered her to the ground. Porcia came over to console her. “First my mother and now my father,” Cassia cried. No one spoke. They gathered around her and hugged her.

“There is war and death here,” said Porcia. “Only the vultures and makers of war, love this sight.” They all got back onto their horses and left, back into the hills.

Once into the hills they stopped for the night near a grove of olives. Getting off their horses, Felix took the horses and hid them further in the grove and came back. “I think it best we make no fire tonight.”

All of them were physically and mentally exhausted and ready to fall and sleep anywhere. Even so, someone had to take watch. Porcia looked a Cassia and her condition, and said, “I’ll a take first watch. We should move eastward in the morning.”

“Alright, I will take second watch till the cocks crow. Where shall we go?” Felix asked his mother.

“Southeastward to my town of Matera. Far away from all of this,” she replied as she slumped to the ground and covered her body with her blanket.

Cassia tossed and turned all night with nightmares, with either Porcia or Felix covering her back up. Morning came and with little to eat and less to say, they moved onward to Matera, the furthest southern part of Italy.

LATE OCTOBER, THE SAME YEAR

Matera village was located high on a large stony, hilltop. Houses clung to the top of the hill and along the sides, with a small defensive wall around the town. Farmers worked the fields below. Sheep and goats walked everywhere, along with donkeys and a few horses. All was quiet. The war seemed very far away and by all accounts, the Vandals and Goths had moved back to wherever they came from in the north, taking all the riches, slaves, and young women they could find.

But on this sunny day, far below the town in an orchard, Cassia, Felix, and Porcia stood side by side with a few local guests off to one side. A priestess dressed in long white robe representing the Goddess of Lares, the protector of households, presided over the ceremony. Cassia wore a long, white, simple dress that a local woman had donated, with a Hercules knot in the center to cover her pregnancy. She had flowers in her hair and a veil over her face. Felix wore a simple, white toga.

The priestess stood before them and the guests. "Your fathers are not here," said the priestess, "so, I will ask your mother, Felix. Porcia, do you allow Felix to marry Cassia?"

Trying not to cry tears of joy, Porcia replied, "Yes, I do."

The priestess turned to Cassia, "What dowry do you hereby give to Felix?"

Cassia smiled widely. "My mother's ring and…" she patted her stomach, "our baby!"

The priestess went on, "Cassia. Do you freely take Felix as your husband for life?"

Cassia looked deeply into Felix's eyes, replying firmly, "Yes, I do."

The priestess looked at Felix. "Felix, do you freely take Cassia as your wife for the rest of your life?"

Felix looked at Cassia. "Yes, I do."

The priestess looked at the guests. "Does anyone here object?" There was laughter and no objection. "Then," said the priestess, "in the eyes of Lares, I pronounce you man and wife."

Felix lifted the veil from Cassia's face and kissed her. She then turned around and with a big smile, threw the flowers high into the air, where the girls behind, failing to catch them, landed on the wall and lay there in the sun.

SEVEN MONTHS LATER

"Theodosius!" Cassia called out from the kitchen where she was washing cups.

"What?" asked Felix from the garden.

"If it's a boy we will call it Theodosius, he will become a great writer and tell of these times."

"And if it's girl?" he called back.

"We will name it after your mother who guided us through those terrible times." Cassia replied through the window.

Felix put down the brick he was about to apply to the new wall and walked back into the kitchen. "What about your mother's name?"

Cassia placed the dry cups into the cupboard. "My mother…we can name the second girl after her."

Felix walked behind Cassia and held her bulging stomach. "So many children we will make?"

Cassia took his hands into hers. "Rome needs babies!"

Felix laughed and kissed her neck. "I'll be too busy being a father to be a senator."

Porcia entered the kitchen, catching the last bit of the conversation. "My son, your Latin still cannot be understood even by these simple neighbors of ours. So, Cassia has sold some of her jewelry and I, my horse for a paedagogia—a slave teacher, for teaching you Latin. You'll never be a senator with your Latin as it is."

Felix sat down and took the water offered by Cassia. "Well, I'm not sure about being a senator anyway, but my son may well be. So! What of Rome?"

Porcia and Cassia sat down opposite him. "It seems that these Vandals wanted to destroy everything beautiful in the city, but it will rise again and your children will be ready to rebuild it!" Porcia replied.

Cassia lifted her glass. "I'll drink to that!" They all clinked glasses, drank, and laughed aloud. "Vivat Roma! Long live Rome!"

End

www.ingramcontent.com/pod-product-compliance
Ingram Content Group UK Ltd.
Pitfield, Milton Keynes, MK11 3LW, UK
UKHW041641190726
13854UKWH00006B/2633

9 781657 240148